Only You: A Bronx Love Story 3

By: Tina Marie

Acknowledgements

I would first like to thank God for giving me this gift of writing and for providing me with every blessing I have received this far and will receive in the future.

I want to thank my family, my fiancé Jay for putting up with all the late nights and my crazy moods while I am writing. To my kids Jashanti, Jaymarni and Jasheer I want you to know that I work so hard so you can have it all. I want to thank all of my Pen Sisters no matter what company you are in for all of the love, support and for always helping to push me to my next goal, I appreciate you all. A special thank you to my new team at SOUL Publications~ the world is ours.

To the crew, my sisters, Sharome, Shante, LaDora, and Andrea I just want to say I love you all and without all the late night calls, test reads, brainstorming, word count challenges and mostly the friendship, without you guys there would be no book so I thank you. When they see y'all they see me and that's how it is!! Nisey Jones I just have to say sis you are the best and I could not leave you out. I appreciate all of the late nights reading my work and giving me feedback. To Chan, Myia and Demettrea you are my sisters now so you are stuck with me for life. Love you ladies.

Thank You Tyanna for being a constant sweetheart and motivator. Author Natavia, you're my sis, my friend, and my favorite author all in one, and I appreciate and love your crazy butt. Nisey Jones, I just have to say, Sis, you're the best. You know my schedule better than me and make me stick to it. I appreciate all of the late nights of reading my work and giving me feedback and for not allowing me to make excuses. Quanisha, you're the best assistant/admin ever. You don't let me forget a thing and handle all the grunt work so I can write. Love you, boo. To Zatasha and all the Bookies I appreciate the love and support you show all authors.

To my friends and family: I appreciate all of the love and support. My cousins, Dionne, Donna & Tanisha. My friends: Letitia, Natasha, Jennifer, Diana and Kia. I'm truly grateful for you all, and I love you. And to my best friend there will never be enough letters in the alphabet to thank you.

To all of our fans, readers, test readers, and anyone who has ever read or purchased my work, shared a link or a book cover, you're all appreciated, and I promise to keep pushing on your behalf to write what you're looking for.

Table of Contents:

Last Time:

Avian

As always anything dealing with Kane is a fucking cause for stress. Looking from him to my mother I was annoyed that they thought I was going to sit down at a dinner with them and play happy fucking family. I was already having a fucked up day, I was with Lena earlier and she admitted she was a pregnant, three months to be exact and the baby was mine. How could I deny it, shit I was hitting that every chance I got. I didn't want to cheat on Za'adore she is just ignorant sometimes, mainly her fly ass mouth made me turn to Lena. Lena is submissive and aims to please me, not argue about every fucking thing.

Glancing once again at my father I couldn't help but wonder when his time would be up, I no longer had any respect for him, especially since he demanded that I give him back Charmayne instead of getting my revenge. I am not big on killing but letting the girl who killed my baby go back to a cozy life made me feel like a straight bitch inside. That was another reason I avoid Za'adore, since I brought Charmayne to my pops and lied to her it feels like whenever I am around her she will guess what I did. Like she could see through a nigga or something. She just stands there shaking her head and rolling her eyes.

"Ok pops I will be here tomorrow night for the dinner you have planned. I doubt I can get Za to come but I will ask." I said as I turned towards the front door to leave.

"Son didn't you tell us last month she was pregnant?" If that is true than you need to bring her, she is carrying an Evans and I need to get to know her better." Kane said the last with a lust filled voice. Shaking my head I left quickly before I punched him in the throat. What a fucking pervert. Shit my girl was carrying his grandkid but all he could think about was looking at her body or trying to fuck her.

Walking in the house an hour later I was dreading the conversation Za'adore and me where about to have. Not seeing her anywhere I checked upstairs and then down. Finally I yanked open the door to the bathroom to see her on her knees throwing up. Holding her hair back for her until she finished I then ran some cold-water on a cool cloth and handed it to her. This pregnancy was almost as bad as the last one. Poor Za didn't want anyone to know she was pregnant again because she said someone would probably try and kill her baby again. I really couldn't argue with her about that shit because I knew that Charmayne was still around.

"Babe my father is throwing a large dinner tomorrow for the family and he would like it if we both attended." As soon as I said the words she was shaking her head no.

"Avian are you fucking stupid? Your father tried to rape me and I am not going to anything with his ass. You can just tell him and the family I said fuck you," she said while throwing herself on the bed and rolling onto her side in a ball. See now I have to show her I was the man and she needed to shut the fuck up and just support me some damn times.

"Hey Za'adore I guess I wasn't really clear on my last statement. The family, my crew, the reason we have all these cars and a nice place to live is having a dinner tomorrow. We will be leaving at five so be ready. This isn't a fucking request it's an order." I walked out of the bedroom door and down to the family room. I needed some time away from her before I hurt my kid while whooping her ignorant ass.

Surprisingly Za'adore ass aint say shit to me the whole rest of the day. She served me dinner and I was sure she even cooked it, while I was eating she got under the table and gave me head. She almost bust her wig open on the marble tabletop when Stacey Ann came into the kitchen unexpectedly. Damn maybe I shouldn't have at the food, her crazy ass probably poisoned me or some other horrific shit.

That night she did the same shit she been doing for a few weeks now, well as least that I noticed when I come to the house was her sitting up in the living room with her face in the phone and the TV on. I wonder what the hell she was really up too. Creeping down the stairs I quietly walked behind the couch she was sitting on. I noticed she had on a silk robe but no other clothes on under it. What the fuck was going on. Snatching the phone right out of her hands she yelled and jumped up to try and grab it back but I moved to fast. If she wasn't pregnant I wouldn't have felt sorry for her when she fell over the back of the couch and hit her ass, hard.

Looking at her screen I could see she was taking pictures of her naked body while she was sitting on the couch. I hurried and clicked to messages only to see some dude sending her pictures of his wrinkled ass dick. This bitch over here having phone sex while I was upstairs trying to think of a way to make her flaky ass happy, I was going to kill her. Seeing the look in my eyes must have scared her ass, she got up and ran to the stairs and almost fell. Taking a deep breath I threw the phone against the wall shattering it. I slowly took the stairs and walked into the room to see Za'adore throwing some clothes in a duffel bag.

"Za'adore where do you think you are going?" I grabbed the bag from her and threw it across the room. "You are possibly carrying my baby so what you will do is get your lying, cheating, sneaking ass into the bed and open those pretty lips so I can treat you like you deserve. You will not leave her until my baby is born and once he or she is in this world and safely with me you can get the fuck out." I grabbed her mouth so hard she had no choice but to open it but as I began rubbing my pre cum over her lips her tears made me stop. My dick went limp and I had to take a seat at the end of the bed. I loved Za and this shit was too much for me to handle right now.

Za'adore

Today was the day we went to the dinner at Kane's house and I have tried to think of any way to back out of it. But since Avian caught me sending Drue naked pictures he has been watching me like white on rice. I guess he thought that nigga was in my purse or something waiting to jump out and fuck me in Kane's living room. I know I was wrong, shit I knew Drue from high school and when I saw him in my Psychology class at college I was just happy to see someone I knew. Then he became someone who was paying me compliments, telling me I was pretty and I looked sexy. He was keeping me company while Avian was out fucking other bitches and doing God knows what else. But I never meant for this shit to go so far.

"Hello," I greeted Kane as we walked in the house and where seated at a long wooden table by who I assumed was a housekeeper. Dinner was Roasted Chicken, Greens, Stuffing, Salad and mashed potatoes. I was scared to eat anything from this house after what happened to me the last time so I just shifted the food around on my plate. Kane and his dad talked about sports and other mundane shit. It was odd that his mother wasn't there but since I was grateful she wasn't I tried to not think her up.

"Honey you didn't tell me you had guests," said an oddly familiar voice. "We were just coming in from the mall and noticed the car parked in the driveway," said Janey as she rounded the corner with a very alive and smiling Charmayne. My fork dropped and I felt like I couldn't breathe. What the hell is my mother doing here with Kane, calling him honey? I must be dead or sleeping because this had to be a dream, I knew that Charmayne's ass was dead because Avian assured me he took care of her. Slowly turning my head I saw a shocked look on Avian's face when he noticed my mother but as soon as he looked at Charmayne his shoulders dropped and his eyes held guilt.

Kemori

Looking at Avian I had to take a deep breath, I turned and looked at the wall and then I turned back. I could feel my fists balling up and my temper was taking over any bit of common sense I was trying to hold on to. I am sure what he just said to me was a fucking joke. I mean what kind of idiot, no I take that back, what kind of weak motherfucker does some shit like that. And once again his fuckshit has trickled down to me only this time it went too far. This time it has gone too far, it has put the woman I love in danger and like always Avian is waiting on me to fix his mistakes and give him what a fucking pat on the back?

"Kem, he didn't mean for this to happen, Kane played all of us, and he and my mother had their own agenda. I was hurt and angry when I found out, shit Nadège is my best friend, like my sister but I know Avian didn't do any of this intentionally, he is not like you, and he has a heart." Za'adore cried out clinging onto my brother's arm like a cheap mink coat. Some best friend she is, I guess when it comes down to it Na really had no one to have her back, it's all about the new nigga and bitch you fucking when it comes to loyalty.

"Look Kem I know that look on your face, we can fix this, don't do anything crazy. You have two kids to think about," he said waving his hand in the direction of Keyon and Kaidence. Like he was motioning to a fucking puppy or something, just real calm and casual after their mother was hurt because of his ass. "I called Kane over here to help us fix this, he can make sure that Cha-,"

Before he could even finish his sentence I punched him in the face so hard I could hear his nose break. Ignoring the crunching sound the beast inside of me wouldn't allow me to stop. "You stupid, pussy mother fucker. You allow these bitches to almost kill you, fine. You allow Kane to ruin your relationship, your life, cool. But when it comes to me and mine I will not allow you to ever FUCK with us again." I roared as I continued to throw blows his way. I could hear Za'adore screaming and pleading but I couldn't focus on anything except breaking open Avian's empty head. I could imagine his brains splattered on the hard wood floor and that was the only thing that would make me happy at the moment. Feeling something scratching my arms I looked down and saw Za'adore hitting me and attempting to pull me off of Avian. Pushing her so hard she flew across the room and landed at Inaya's feet I went back to the task at hand. Finally Avian's body was lying before me, broken and bloody. Hearing someone clapping I turned around only to find Kane standing behind me with a smirk on his face, he stood clapping his hands like this was some fucking movie that he watched and enjoyed.

I could still replay the moment a few hours ago when Angalee admitted to stalking Na and then showed me the picture of Charmayne running my girl down outside the doctor's office. I finally snapped and hurt Angalee, it had been a long time coming. Shit I may have even hurt our baby but my mind was overrun with anger and I couldn't control it. Avian got to his feet like an old man and his eyes were staring at me with so much intensity I almost forgot why I was there, almost forgot he was my brother and not some nigga in the street.

"Why Kane, I know you did this shit, I am your son, just like Avian is your fucking son why," I asked? I knew he was behind this, just like he was behind my spot getting robbed the other day. He has always had it out for me but has never wanted to explain why. I bet today he would be explaining some shit. I was sorry I brought my kids to Avian's house because now I felt like this shit was not even safe for me. Avi's bitch ass was looking like a Pit-bull ready to lock on some shit and Kane had a devious smile on his face. "Avian really son you let Charmayne go after she poisoned your girl, killed your baby," I said reminding him of how fucked up this shit was.

"It was because you were born Kemori that was what Kane had against you. See it was never about Kane not wanting more children it was because when you were born it kept him from marrying the woman he really loved. I was about to give Kane his divorce until I found out he was sleeping with your mother. If you would not have been born I would not have found out and Kane would have moved on with his little Puerto Rican Princess and your sister wouldn't have been a bastard. So he hates you because you ruined his life." Explained Avian's dough faced ass mother.

Stacey Ann stood in the corner shaking her head no like she was convincing herself or going crazy. All these years she thought she was the love of his life, shit I guess not. Monica looked at her with so much hate I was surprised my mom didn't catch on fire. "Za'adore I like you, you remind me a lot of me at your age, ready to fight my situation and not give up. Please do not think Charmayne is the reason your baby is dead. Had I known you were poisoned I would have told you who did it a long time ago. The reason Stacey Ann and Kemori had to leave Kane's home was not because I found out she was his mistress, I been knew that shit. It was because she was poisoning me."

Za'adore looked at Stacey Ann and began to run towards her. I pulled out my gun at the same time as Avian and Kane. "Pop" was all you heard in the room then silence

Chapter 1-Every time I close my eyes

Kemori

Looking around the room to make sure my brother was good I saw him with his gun still pointed in my direction. "Avi, you good son? I know you pissed but stop pointing that fucking thing my way," I said letting him know whatever beef we had was over for the moment. When I heard those shots all I thought about was making sure his ass was good. I had already peeped Inaya leaving with my kids when the arguing first started. No matter what at the end of the day my brother was all I had. Plus I was just used to being his protector, always had been.

"Yea me and Za are good," He responded as he put the gun to his side. Za was tucked behind his back, holding onto Avian like a second skin. I guess I was happy nothing happened to Za. I didn't want Nadège to fuck me up about her best friend even though Za ass got all the way on my fucking nerves. Letting my eyes roam around the room I noticed my uncle was standing there literally holding a smoking gun. He was looking down at my pops with some wild ass look in his eyes. Kane was slowly bleeding all over the floor. I wanted to feel something besides relief and a sense of joy, but I couldn't. He struggled to speak while holding his hand up to his chest. His mouth was open and flopping around like a fish in low water. I was interested in what his last words were going to be. I walked closer to him with my gun in my hand. Damo was pacing the floor and looking over at Kane every few seconds. His muttering to himself was getting annoying.

"Damo what the fuck is wrong with you," I asked? "You started this shit now finish him off, I got stuff to do." I was ready to get this shit wrapped up so I could go home to my family. "Hey pops, speak up nigga we can't hear you." I laughed as I kicked my dad in his ribs. He tried to play tough and not show the pain he was in but human nature took over and he began coughing up blood.

Suddenly he looked up with so much fury in his eyes I stepped back. Following his gaze I realized it went to my mother. "No, you killed him Damo. Why would you do that to him? Kane I love you, you can't die," she sobbed as she made her way closer. This bitch was delusional, didn't she see he hated her. I'm assuming he always did, aside from pussy she was nothing else to him. She was just a young fuck.

Kane's body began to shake but he sat up, he was fighting what was supposed to be a for sure death. Leave it to this dude to try and outrun the grim reaper. Not on my watch though. Picking up my gun I aimed at his head. "No final words, *Dad*," I said sarcastically. He was never really my father, hell no one was. The streets raised me.

"I'm not your father you little bastard. He is," he said pointing at Damo. I felt like a building fell on me at his revelation. I knew he wasn't going to lie on his death bed. I could see the truth in his eyes. So that was why he always hated me, beat me and did anything to make my life hell. Seeing my shock he began to laugh. It was a loud grating laugh, one that men used to make other men feel small. I couldn't help it if I tried. Even though I wanted more information from Kane the rage inside of me couldn't be tamed.

Walking closer I could no longer hear anything around me. It was like the world was on mute. I could see Damo stop pacing and his mouth was moving. My bitch of a mother must have been screaming. Her body language gave it away. None of it mattered. None of it would change the outcome. I counted my steps to stay focused on the task before me. One, two, three, four and then I was there, leaning in front of Kane. I looked into his eyes as he coughed up more blood. It was all over his mouth and shirt. I lifted the gun to the middle of his head and pulled the trigger. I watched his soul leave his body as my face was splattered with his brains. At that moment I felt nothing, just blank like I had never felt an emotion in my life.

Standing, I suddenly felt something pinch my side. Quickly turning I pulled the trigger several times. Avi's mother dropped to the floor still holding the kitchen knife she used to stab me in my left side. "I loved him," she whispered before her body relaxed and her breathing could no longer be heard. Looking at Avian I wasn't sure what to expect. I had just killed both of his parents and found out I wasn't his brother after all. He looked at me and shook his head in understanding. He looked like a burden was lifted from him. I guess with parents like those all you could feel was relief.

"How could you kill your father Kemori, I knew you were the devil. I wanted to abort you the second I found out I was pregnant. I knew that you would ruin my life. The life I was building with Kane. He saw the evil in you. He tried everything to get it out. He beat you, starved you and gave you tough love. He didn't deserve this." She went off on me. Her normally put together hair was on end and her house coat was wrinkled. The tears were streaming down her bloodshot eyes.

Was this what men did to women, or was this what women did to men? Either way I made a decision at that moment. It was time to let go of Nadège once and for all. Look at the monster my parents created. I didn't want my children to become monsters, like me. I watched as the blood oozed from my side. The person who should have cared about me the most was too busy grieving the man who made me this way. "We gotta clean this shit up ourselves," I told Avian motioning to the two dead bodies.

Damo walked towards my mother and used the back of his hand to slap her. It was so loud everyone left in the house stopped to stare. Her eyes got wide and her body was still. I wondered at that moment what her parents were like. Who made her, someone so spiteful, hateful? She called me the devil, but the devil was really in her. Damo lifted her over his shoulder like she was a bag of laundry or trash. "Nooo," she screamed and began bucking her body trying to get loose. Her legs were flailing against his shoulders but Damo wasn't even fazed. "Shut up, I told you the first day I saw your ass you belonged to me," he told Stacey Ann. His voice sounded strange, almost like he was possessed or something. Walking right out the front door he didn't even look back as he took who he came for.

Going to the downstairs bathroom I grabbed a towel to push against the gaping cut in my side. It burned like hell but it wasn't the first time I had been through some shit like this. "Son you good," Phantom asked as I headed for the door. Hitting him with a head nod I waited until we were both outside before I spoke.

"I'm about to go to Angalee's crib and have someone come take care of this shit. Go to the house and make sure my family is aight." I had one hand on the door of my whip waiting on him to confirm. I could see by the look on his face he felt some type of way about my plans. Honestly though I didn't give a fuck. I always been the kind of nigga who did what the fuck he wanted despite what people thought.

"Son you fucking tripping, you running to that crazy bitch Angalee even though she is the cause of so many of your problems? You got a good as girl at home. She's probably worried about your punk ass but you running to the next bitch. What am I supposed to tell shorty when I walk in there alone? Man Inaya is going to give me hell for this shit." Phantom gave me the evil eye and shook his head. Climbing in his truck he peeled out leaving me standing there. Maybe he was right, I should just go home to Na and our kids. Feeling the blood from my side leak out of the towel I could feel the wet stickiness on my fingers.

Fuck I couldn't go home to my girl looking like this. She was already stressed out and didn't need to deal with anything else. Besides I made a decision to leave Nadège alone, I just had to get my heart on board. Picking up the phone I dialed a number I thought I would never be using again. "Hello," she answered in a low voice. She was either sleeping or crying from the ass whooping I gave her earlier.

"Angalee come to my house now. I need you to help me with something." I hung up and didn't give her a chance to respond. Fuck it I wasn't going to make it all the way to her place plus I wanted to be comfortable in my own shit. The ride home was longer than I wanted, the loss of blood had me feeling dizzy as fuck and there were moments I almost blacked out on the expressway. Pulling up I saw Angalee waiting on the doorstep, I could tell by the look on her face she was surprised to see me so soon.

"Ang how the fuck you get over here so fast," I asked with doubt on my face. I called her twenty minutes ago and she at lease lived an hour from my crib. She backed up slowly until she had nowhere to go and her back was against the front door. That was when I noticed the crow bar in her hand. Jerking my head to the driveway I saw the windows shattered on my Range Rover. "Bitch," I called out as I bounded up the stairs forgetting all about my stab wound. Grabbing her by those twists she always wore I yanked her closer to me.

"Avian I'm sorry. I didn't mean to do it. It's this pregnancy that has me crazy. When you pushed me down I was so hurt. I wanted to get back at you. I promise I will pay to get it fixed." She begged as I tightened my grip. I could see the hair straining her scalp. It was always something with this bitch. Hell her pussy wasn't even that fucking good.

"You sure the fuck will. Now follow me I inside and stitch this cut up. I got shit to do." Her eyes got wide as she looked at my wound. I didn't know if she wanted to throw up or faint but I knew her ass could do it. She used to be a nurse before she started doing whatever the fuck it was she did now. Sitting on a chair in the kitchen I watched as she gathered shit she could use from the bathroom.

"Babe you ok? Who did this to you?" She asked as she cut my shirt off of me and poured peroxide over the wound. I had to grit my teeth after that. I think I even passed out for a few minutes. I knew I should have gone to a hospital but fuck it. It was a kitchen knife and not that deep. Once the final piece of thread was stitched in I let out the breath I didn't know I was holding. "Let me put some gauze on this and you should be good as new." She had the nerve to lean down and kiss me on the cheek.

"Aright thanks," I stood up and lightly stretched making sure I could still move. Reaching in my pocket I threw her a few hundred dollars and walked to the front door. "Good looking out Ang," I opened the door letting her know her time was up. She looked at me with her lips poked out and tears in her eyes. I nudged her gently until she was on the doorstep then slammed the door in her face.

Nadège

When the nurse came in to the room I really didn't pay much attention to anything she said except I was lucky. That was my cue to get the fuck out of this hospital bed. After the last time I spent laid up I knew I couldn't do that shit no more. "Nurse I would like my discharge papers," I told her sitting up to get my clothes. I shot Kem a text telling him I was checking myself out. He didn't respond but it said he read it. I knew he was going to see his brother today so I didn't take it personal.

"Ma'am, the doctor would like to keep you one more night for observation." She said in one of those voices you use to convince a small child to do some unwanted task.

"Look I know you are trying to be caring and are just doing your job but I need my discharge papers now. I don't need to be patronized. I was hit by a car. I feel like shit, but I can get up and move around so I can feel like shit in my own place." She gave me a dirty look and mumbled something under her breathe. Had I been in the mood I would have checked her but my head was not feeling great and I just wanted to leave. Twenty minutes later I was walking my ass to the front door to catch a Taxi home. I could have called for a ride but if Kem was in the Bronx it would have took him too long.

I was at home for a few hours before Inaya came rushing in the house with the kids and no Kemori I suddenly felt sick to my stomach. "Inaya what the fuck is going on, are the kids ok, Kem" I asked in a panic?

"Na please have a seat, your ass is pacing back and forth looking like a wounded puppy. Phantom is still there, I just left because Kem and his brother were arguing. Actually Kem was raising his voice and Avi was whining. I am sure he will be back soon, probably as aggy as ever." She seemed so sure of what she was saying. She didn't look worried at all. But there was just this feeling that something was wrong. A feeling I couldn't shake.

Inaya and I watched some scorned lover type movies on Life Time while Keyon played until he fell asleep on the living room floor. Still no Kemori and it was getting dark outside. I was checking my phone for what felt like the hundredth time when Phantom came strolling through the front door. Expecting Kem to be coming in behind him my heart started racing when he closed and locked the door, alone. He opened his mouth to speak but I just held up my hand and shook my head. I had been texting and calling Kem for hours and nothing. Seeing Phantom let me know he was alright, just not fucking with me. I wanted to be mad at Phantom but it wasn't his fault that Kem was being a dick.

Standing Keyon up I made him walk up the stairs. Slowly we made our way to my bedroom. I was still sore from Charmayne's ass hitting me with her car. That was one thing I respected about Kem. He didn't hide certain things from me. Once he found out who hit me he told me what was up right away. He even told me how Angalee was stalking me and how he fucked her up. I knew Charmayne would come up dead sooner than later because unlike his brother, my baby-father handled his business.

I put both kids in bed with me while wiping my tears. Seeing Inaya had trailed behind me I hated that she had to see me breaking down like this. "I'm fine, just get some sleep," I said. She looked at me a few more minutes before she turned and made her way further into my room.

"I know you on some I hate Kem and I am going to cry about it type shit. But trust me, the best revenge on a man who is acting up is finding your own happiness. Don't let the shit he doing mess wit' your head even if it is messing wit' your heart. I remember going through so much with Phantom, hell when I was pregnant with our son his ass disappeared to a whole other state. Then came back and got a girlfriend, some old busted bitch. It broke me down a lot. During that time the one thing I learned was that I had to just love me. If Phantom was going to be the one or not I had to love myself."

"I know I am just so hurt, even though we not together right now he could at least acknowledge my calls and shit. I mean what if there was an emergency, I got his kids over here and he acting like I am just some random hoe calling." I sighed in frustration while sinking back onto my fluffy pillows. Placing my head in my hand all I could think about was what Inaya said. Did I love me, could I even love me? I mean hell my mother and father couldn't love me, I think a part of me just felt like I wasn't worthy of my own love because of that.

She leaned over and hugged me before she left out of the room. I turned off the bedside lamp and tucked the covers around Keyon. The baby was sleeping peacefully in her bassinet with one fist in her mouth. Kaidence was Kemori's twin. She had his eyes, lips and even made the same facial expressions as him. I loved my kids so much, Inaya was right. I had to get my head together, if not for me than for them.

Before I knew it the day had caught up to me and my eyes were heavy. Suddenly I didn't know where I was, it was pitch black and all I could hear was my heart beating in my ears. It sounded like water rushing by. I could see Sam standing over me, he had my arms pinned down and his hands began roaming my body. No, this couldn't be happening to me again, why wouldn't Sam just die already? I tried to scream but no sounds were coming out of my mouth. Sam began laughing then his face changed, he started looking like someone else, like Kane.

His thick hands wrapped around my neck cutting off my air supply. He was laughing at me and every time I struggled his laugh got louder. I reached up to scratch his eyes out when I felt someone shaking me. "Na wake up, it's ok," I sat straight up and saw Kem standing next to the bed. I felt the sweat dripping down my neck and my body was shaking. He carefully stroked my hair and rubbed my back. As soon as I saw him I knew my feeling was right, something was wrong with Kem. Instead of jumping down his throat asking for information I remained quiet. Watching as he removed his bloody clothes I sucked in a sharp breathe as I noticed the bandages on his side.

He walked to the bathroom and I heard the shower turn on. It wasn't the bandage or the ripped and blood stained clothes that worried me. It was the look on his face. He looked like he was in shock. There was no emotion there, nothing. He came out wrapped in a towel. His movements were slow as he put on clean boxers and a t-shirt. He climbed in the bed next to me and still had not spoken. It took every bit of will power not to ask him what the fuck was going on. He ran his hands over Keyon's braids and gently touched Kaidence's cheek.

Pulling me close he buried his face in my neck. I could feel him tense up for a moment. I assumed my body hit his wound. Suddenly I felt wetness trickling onto my skin. They were Kemori's tears. Turning around so we were face to face I wrapped my arms around him. Holding him close, I whispered in his ear, "Kemori, its ok, whatever it is we will get through it." In that moment all of the bullshit we had been through in the past few months faded away. My love for Kem was too deep to be ignored and I knew at this moment he needed me.

"Kane wasn't really my father," he blurted out. "All of that time, shit all those years I spent wondering why he didn't love me. Why he refused to claim me. Hell I even blamed him for fucking up my mother, looks like his brother was responsible for that." He took a deep breath before he continued to tell me everything that happened at Avian's house. My blood ran cold once I found out he was stabbed. Rubbing my hands up and down his back I wished I could kill Kane all over again, and his bitch ass mother too. I hoped Damo tortures her in the worst way possible. Hearing that he kidnapped her was amusing to me. Karma at its best, maybe he would feed her a little antifreeze the way she was giving it to my best friend. It was her fault Za'adore changed. Stacey Ann killed Za's baby and my friend would never be the same. Maybe I should have killed her ass. I was always sitting around playing the victim. Watching people do things to me or the ones I loved but never doing a thing about it. I think it was time for that to change.

I felt Kem's breathing even out and realized he had fallen asleep. "Lord please watch over my family. I don't know what storm is coming or how much more we can take." I prayed out loud hoping God would hear my pleas. This past year had been crazy and the last time I went through a cycle like this, well it didn't end well.

Before the sun was up so was Kem, he fed the baby a bottle while gazing at her like he would never see her again. My anxiety felt like it was going to consume me. "Kem I know you, what you told me last night isn't all. There was something you were holding back from me." I tried to talk to him but he just ignored me and kept feeding Kaidence. Once she fell back asleep he carried Keyon to his room. I was silently thankful because as much as I loved my son nearby he slept like a wild hyena. Kem was gone so long I almost went looking for him.

The clock on my cable box read four a.m., the luminous blue numbers blurred as I tried to keep my tired eyes open. I just began to get back into a deep sleep when Kem got back in the bed. "Come here," he said in a voice that was unlike his normal one. His tone was low and filled with sadness. As soon as he lightly touched my arms with his fingertips my body came to life. I started kissing his lips and he lightly bit mine. I slipped out of Kems t-shirt I wore to bed and had on only my red silk panties.

I could tell he was trying not to hurt the cut in his side so I decided to help him. Pulling his dick out of his boxers I began stroking him with my hands. Wiggling down on the bed I licked the head of his cock and moaned at the same time as he did. I made sure to take him to the back of my throat the way I knew he liked it. I felt his hand tangle in my hair and push my head down further. I wanted to gag but held it down and gave Kem the best fucking head of his life. I could taste his pre-cum as it oozed out of his dick. I pulled back and licked the head until he just couldn't take it anymore.

"Give me this pussy girl," he growled as he pulled my body across his. My juices leaked everywhere as I felt the tip of his dick at my entrance. He suckled my breasts, first gently than with passion. He pushed up forcing his way inside of my tight hole. "Ahhh, yes girl fuck me back," he moaned as I rode him. Forgetting about everything else but how he felt deep inside of me I couldn't stop. He grabbed my face and looked deep in my eyes. His lips met mine and it was so intense. "I will always love you," he said over and over again in between kisses.

"Kemori I am going to cum," I yelled out. He grabbed my ass and sank my body into his harder. Feeling him go deeper I was so turned on I couldn't stop but to squirt all over his dick. He groaned in my ear and his nails dug into my flesh as I felt his nut shoot inside of me. I rolled over onto my side and fell back to sleep as soon as I felt Kem's arms around me.

Chapter 2- The making of a man

Avian

I slowly cleaned up my parents remains. I wrapped them in a tarp I kept in the basement and loaded their bodies in the trunk. My pops rolled in first with a thud, then my mom on top of him. Slamming the trunk closed I realized I didn't feel much of anything, just numb. Like someone put a blanket over my head and I was walking around unaware. As much as I wanted to call someone to come do this shit for me, for once I was going to listen to Kem and handle the bodies myself. Looking around the living room I just shook my head. There was blood everywhere. Some from the murder victims and the rest from my broken nose, I was fucking Kem up as soon as I saw him for that shit. I was too sexy to have a fucked up nose.

Za'adore walked back in the room wearing some old ass stained up sweat suit and thick yellow gloves on. She had all her wild ass hair tied up with a scarf. I could smell the bleach in the bucket next to her. Shit I was thankful she was looking out for a nigga and cleaning up. She was on her hands and knees with a scrub brush putting in work. Looking up I knew some slick shit was about to slither out of that pretty mouth. "So you just standing there watching me nigga, you want me to dispose of the bodies too," she asked with sarcasm? The way she rolled her eyes at me like I was trash made me feel like less of a man. It took all of my self-control to not snatch her up.

"Fuck you Za'adore, I have had enough of yo ass. You just don't learn, but I bet the hell you will soon. Just clean this shit up, and Za one more thing. You look better on your knees." I laughed as she threw the bloody sponge my way. She folded her arms across her small baby bump and grilled me as I slammed the front door to go handle my business. Deciding to make this a threesome I drove for a while until I pulled up to the gates of my father's house. If I was going to be out here playing cremator I might as well add Charmayne to the list. I noticed the gate was slightly opened and I didn't see a body guard around. That was strange. Driving in slowly I kept my hand on my nine and my eyes on my surroundings. Something here felt wrong but I wasn't leaving without who I came for.

Parking I got out and noticed Zeke and Mane on the front lawn leaking. Even the dogs my pops kept around were sprawled on the grass with bullet holes all over their bodies. It looked like whoever shot them was either really pissed or had no idea what the fuck they were doing. Slipping into the house through a side entrance I walked as quietly as I could. The pictures on the wall were smashed, some lying on the floor. What the fuck happened here. Rounding the corner as soon as my foot hit the bottom step I heard the laughter. "Ooh baby right there," a woman half giggled and half moaned. Spinning around I walked in their direction instead.

I have never wanted to cover my eyes at the site of something so much. Charmayne and Za'adores mother were on the couch kissing each other and sharing a bottle of Henny straight to the head. These bitches had on silk robes and expensive looking heels. Charmayne had her robe opened and Za'adore's mother was trailing her hands across her legs and back to her wet pussy. These hoes were in here having a fucking freak session obvious to everything going on around them. They were either too fucked up to notice what was up or they had something to do with all the dead bodies outside. Stepping out of the shadows Charmayne gasped in surprise once she saw my face. I slowly walked over to the ladies as they scrambled to cover their bodies with the flimsy robes they had on.

Grabbing Charmayne by her hair I couldn't believe I let her live this long. "Bitch get on your knees," I demanded yanking her to the ground. Za'adore's mother looked calm as a damn cucumber. I guess she thought this shit had nothing to do with her so she was safe.

"Please don't kill us, I am pregnant with your baby," cried Charmayne. Shaking my head at her I laughed. She was really trying to salvage her worthless life. Placing my gun to her head she began to scream. It was loud and grating. Pulling the trigger for the first time I was hyped to kill someone. Looking at the hole in her head I felt like a weight was lifted off my back. For the first time I enjoyed the kill, I could feel the adrenaline rushing through my body. Za'adore's mother was cowering on the couch, she was scooting back so far it looked like the pillows were swallowing her.

"Don't bother trying to run, where you hiding? You think that couch is turning into a space ship and about to fly you out of here? Don't even open that mouth over there smelling like Charmayne pussy. I wouldn't let you live anyway but I wanted to make it clear before I end your worthless life why. You are going to die because you're a shitty mother. No other way around it. You hurt Za so much, damaged her so badly and I love her so you my friend got to go." I laughed a little as I shot out both of her eyes. She was crying and the tears mixed with her blood. I wonder if she thought about her daughter as her life flashed before her eyes. Fuck it. I pulled my parents bodies in the house and made a pile on the floor. I poured the Henny over the bodies lit a match and walked out of the house. I hoped every bit of it burned to the fucking ground.

I sat in the truck watching the flames for a while until I heard the sirens in the distance. Pulling off my phone rang back to back. Lena and Za'adore called me but I ignored them all. I took the long way home and pulled up to Za'adore waiting on the doorway. "Charmayne is taking care of," I said as I brushed by her and made my way upstairs. She followed close behind as I made my way into my bedroom. Turning around fast I flung out my arm and she almost fell over.

"Where you think you going? I thought I made it clear since you a hoe yo ass sleeps in the guest room." I stood still blocking her way as she looked at me like I was confused.

"But with everything that happened I just thought-"

"Yo B you thought wrong. Go take all that thinking in the fucking guest room and leave me alone. I'm good over here." I slammed the door in her face and locked it behind me. When she betrayed me by fucking with that other nigga I stopped giving a fuck about her situations.

Za'adore

I didn't know how I felt about all the shit that had been going on around me. I never knew that the man who was the closest thing I had to a father was, well crazy for lack of a better word. It seemed like everything that touched this family turned to shit. Sitting down on the front step I looked up at the clouds. It had been two days since Avian watched his mother and father murdered and he had been silent. Well after he told me to get the fuck out his space and slammed doors in my face and shit. I had no idea what was going on in his head but I did know that he was feeling some type of way. He had not slept in the bed with me since he caught me sexting Drue. But I thought after I helped clean up a murder scene in his crib he would have showed me some love. Avian always took shit too far and it was really working my nerves. With this pregnancy I was super horny and my vibrator was getting old, fast. All this selfish ass nigga had to do was throw some dick my way. I didn't need no cuddles or shit like that just some good D.

I still couldn't believe I was pregnant again. With Charmayne finally dead for real this time and Stacey Ann's sick ass gone I should finally feel relief. Sadly I didn't. All the stress was crashing down on me at once. It had been a long ass year this was one for the books. Catching a whiff of a neighbor baking an apple pie it made me miss my old life. When my mother would win big at whatever gambling spot she had frequented, she always came home and made me a fresh apple pie. Before I came here I lived in a roach infested apartment in the Bronx. I was destined to become a young mother, high school dropout or just another around the way girl. Somehow I made it out, to the suburbs of Long Island with a rich baby daddy. But it didn't feel like a success.

Laughing up at the sky I felt crazy. All the money in the world couldn't buy comfort or the security that came with a routine, even if it was a bad one. I missed lying in my bed with my pink curtains blowing in the breeze. Waiting on Nadège to get off of work and come hang out with me. Now I didn't even have my best friend to talk to. All I had was whatever drama that was sure to come next. Avian pulled in the driveway, swerving as he rammed the car into park. I could hear the grinding of the Porsche's gears. He stumbled out with bloodshot eyes and an almost empty bottle of Henny in his hand. "Hey baby," he slurred as he grabbed my breast with his free hand.

I noticed he smelled like some type of fruity perfume and the zipper on his jeans were opened. Shaking my head I flung his hand off of me. "Avian you need to get yourself together, call Kem if you need to. Maybe your brother can help you." I was interrupted by him violently grabbing my chin. Looking in his eyes I wasn't scared of the man I saw before me. His eyes showed me all the pain he had carried with him his entire life. Pain he had shoved deep down inside trying to be a son that Kane didn't appreciate. That pain was there now, front and center and Avian couldn't deal with it.

"Kemori's not my fucking brother. I lived in his shadow all these years for nothing. He was just some bastard cousin. I protected him when no one wanted him. I was a good brother to him." He started out angry but ended sad. I knew it was the liquor talking. I had been around enough drunk and angry men in my life to understand that. Besides ever since he watched his father get murdered Avian has drank every day. That liquor was catching up to him.

"Avian, go sleep it off, or go back to your bitches house. Whatever works for you, but leave me the hell alone." I snatched my chin from his fingers and went back in the house. I expected him to follow, but he never came. A little while later I heard him screech his tires as he went back to wherever he came from.

Avian didn't come home for days. I had money and Sophie's new nanny Miss Peary was a doll but I missed Avian. Plus I needed some dick. Clicking on *Hubby* in my phone I called him but he didn't answer. Fuck that this nigga needed to climb out of the funky pussy he was swimming in and pick up the damn phone. I dialed his number at least thirty times back to back before his punk ass finally picked up. "Yo why the fuck is you calling my shit like that," he said sounding annoyed as hell.

"Avian, you have a woman at home, you have a daughter and baby on the way. Bring your black ass home now. I have been silent long enough and if you are not home in the next two hours some other man will be in our bed." I screamed into the phone, I was sure I sounded hysterical but I had enough of this. I just wasn't here for it. Not today. I knew Avi's crazy ass was on the way so I hurried my prego ass to the shower. I guess he was closer than I thought because I was only under the hot spray for about ten minutes before he barged in. He stepped in the walk in shower with his clothes still on and snatched me out with soap still on my skin.

"You going to have who in my bed," he asked with a lot of bass in his voice. I was turned on. I missed this side of Avian. The man with authority and a back bone. Rolling my eyes I placed my hand on his jeans. Making my way to his dick I wasn't surprised when it immediately rocked up. I knew he missed this pussy. Licking my lips I smiled slyly and moved closed to Avi. He still had his hands in my hair but his grip had loosened. "Za what the hell are you doing to me?" It was more a statement instead of a question.

I snaked my arms around his neck and began kissing his jaw. I kissed all over his face until his lips met mine. Swirling my tongue around his I became lost in Avian, in his sexiness, in his presence. "Avi I want you," I cried out as he began sucking on my exposed breasts. My nipples were so thick and full due to my pregnancy. They were also sensitive and with every flick of his tongue or brush of his lips my whole body was on fire. Unconsciously the lower half of my body began to grind into him. Begging for his touch or something more, like feeling him fill me up. His hand slid down my leg and flicked over my swollen nub.

I drew in a sharp breathe because the feeling was so good. I held my body stiff waiting for him to touch my clit once again. I needed to feel his hands on me. When he took too long I guided him back to my pussy. It didn't take much. Hell Avian knew my body better than I did. He began tugging on my clit while he slid first one finger than a second into my tight hole. I pulled at his shirt until the buttons flew off. He slid it onto the floor followed by his pants. I stood before him naked, shivering on the outside from not drying off but burning with desire inside.

Suddenly his warmth was gone as he pulled his pants back on and walked away from me. He looked at me as if he suddenly remembered something. He shook his head and began mumbling to himself as he turned to walk out of the bathroom. "Avian, what the fuck are you doing," I yelled out in frustration? I was naked, pussy and body wetter than Niagara Falls and this fucker was walking away. Nah it wasn't going down like that. I picked up a full shampoo bottle and threw it at Avi's head. I laughed out loud once I heard the thud as it hit him. Right on fucking target.

"Za'adore what the hell is your problem. You keep pushing me and pushing me. I have been trying not to beat the fucking baby out your ass. I am not fucking you. I may be drunk as hell but you not tricking me into running in that corrupted pussy." His eyes looked me up and down like you would something that was disgusting. I knew he was still mad at me. He never got over me sending sex messages to Drue. We have only had sex one time since then and he acted like I was forcing him.

Picking up the conditioner I threw that next. Watching as it hit him in the chest I grabbed my towel off the sink. "Avian, fuck you and your little ass dick, like I said on the phone I have no problem finding another man to come dick me down." The conditioner must have been opened because the thick white liquid had leaked onto his designer jeans and the floor. He turned to come after me but slipped on the wet floor were the water had mixed with the conditioner. He flew face forward onto the floor and hit his head on the counter with a thud. The look on his face was pure rage. He didn't even seem drunk anymore.

Avian began to lift himself off the ground and I knew he was going to fuck me up. Slowly I backed up towards the door. Once I felt the frame I turned and ran. I almost fell on the stairs but somehow I managed to keep my balance and get to the front door.

"You better run bitch," Avian yelled down the stairs as he followed behind me. I swung open the front door and glimpsed Miss Peary standing in the front hall with her mouth opened wide. Seeing the same expression on our neighbors face as my feet hit the concrete I realized I must have dropped my towel on my way out. Looking around I had to think fast so I decided to go hide in the garage. I spent hours in there, shaking from the cool air and my lack of clothes. I was surprised someone didn't call the cops when they saw me run outside naked and scared.

Finally I heard Avian's car door slam, I made my way to peer out of the door and make sure he was gone. Only then did I make my way back inside. This time I made sure to take my ass to the guest room.

Chapter 3- It's so hard to say good-bye
Kemori

After I made love to Nadège I sat up the rest of the night watching her sleep. She was sprawled across my chest, the thousand count sheets where sliding off her hips giving me a view of her bare ass. I swear I could just stay in this bed and fuck her all day. Leaving Na wasn't going to be easy. I was leaving my heart, my comfort. Shit the only comfort I ever really had. I didn't want to do this but I had too. I slowly eased off the bed. I felt like I was sneaking around. Like a kid who was doing something wrong. I walked in the closet and grabbed two of the Adidas duffel bags I had on the shelf. I opened the safe I had in the corner and looked at the money and paperwork that was in there. Looking up I made sure I could still hear her even breathing. I made sure the papers where all there, stocks, insurance and the titles to my cars and properties.

I knew everyone thought I was a dumb thug. Out here hustling for Jordan's and Beamers. That was the furthest thing from the truth. I always knew that my pops, well Kane would never help me if shit went left. So I made sure I could back up my money, have something to fall back on when this hustling shit someday went bust. Now that I had kids it was all for them, that was why I was leaving this shit with Nadège. I took stacks of wrapped hundred dollar bills and removed them from my safe to Na's. I didn't know how she was going to take me leaving her for good but I wanted to make sure she was straight.

I took the clothes I had hanging in the closet and started throwing them in the duffel bags on the floor. I knew I couldn't take everything in one trip but I would just come back for the rest. I could feel her eyes on me, watching me as I packed. She didn't say a word, just leaned against the doorframe. Her eyes were narrowed into slits and followed my every move. I was stuck on what I should say. Did I get mad at her for something she didn't do? I could make up a mystery man or rumors of her cheating. That way I had an excuse to leave. Then it wouldn't be on me. Finally I zipped the bags shut. Grabbing my gun out of the lock box I put it in my waist and got ready to leave. Bending down to kiss my baby I felt Nadège mush me in my face.

"Yo what the fuck is your problem," I hissed? I was trying to remain calm and not wake up my princess.

"Kemori Evans you are my fucking problem! You just come home all stabbed up acting strange. Fuck me, wake up a few hours later and pack your shit to leave?" She slapped the shit out of me as soon as I straightened up from the bassinet. "Kem fuck you, if you leave this time don't fucking come back." She was screaming and shit but not crying. I could see the rage in her eyes. I guess I pushed her past her breaking point.

"Man shut the fuck up before you wake up my baby. I don't have to explain what I am doing to you. We was not together I just been here with my kids. Making sure you was good with the baby and shit. Now I am leaving so back the fuck off. I'm out." I tried to walk out of the room but she charged at me and shoved me so hard I fell into the baby's bassinet almost knocking it over. Kaidence's screams could be heard throughout the room. Na lifter her arm to hit me again, only this time she had a bottle of perfume clutched in her fist. Grabbing her wrist mid-air she dropped the bottle on the floor.

"Just get the fuck out. Remember what I said about not coming back. You are a loser. You are always hiding behind whack ass excuses and saying shit like we not together anyway. So you was just here for your kids while you was living up in my pussy every day? Telling me how much you love me?" Shaking her head she grabbed our daughter in one hand and began calming her down. Her ass lucky baby girl was just startled and not hurt. "What the fuck you still standing there for?" She yelled. She began using her free hand to remove some clothes I had in a drawer and carrying them into the bathroom. I smelled bleach before I walked out of the bedroom. Damn Nadège was wild when she was ready. I knew she wouldn't take it well but she didn't deserve a monster like me.

Throwing my shit in the trunk of my BMW I jogged back in to the house and threw the keys to the Infinity truck on the table. Na needed a truck now with both kids. Locking up I started up my car and sat in the driveway for a few minutes. I thought I would feel better after this shit, feel free. But instead I felt worse. Seeing my phone ring I hoped it wasn't Nadège calling to cuss my ass out again I was tired of fighting with her. Seeing Boon calling I picked up. "What's up son," I said into the speaker?

"Nigga we got to have a family meeting son. I been trying to link Avian but when he did answer he sounded like he was lit. They found ya'll pops in his crib wit three women. They were all shot then burned to death. That shit looked horrible man. Come meet me on 161st son so we can pull this shit together." Boon was rambling on and on. I knew that nigga thought it was me that offed Kane. Hell I was wondering who burned the house to the ground and who the fuck this other dead bitches were.

"Aright son let me try and get my hands on Avian and I will come through," I told him before I clicked the off button disconnecting the call. Why every time some crazy shit happen all eyes was on me. Pulling out of the driveway I rolled down the street and lit up a blunt. I needed to smoke more than ever. Hopping on the I80 I made my way back to the Bronx.

Nadège

I tossed and turned most of the night. I kept having the same nightmare over and over again. The one that started with Sam raping me and his face turned into Kane's. He was leering over me, smirking, as he came closer and closer. His thick hands would wrap around my neck and I couldn't breathe. That is when I would wake up, jumping up out of my sleep. Except this time Kemori wasn't there to comfort me. Each time I woke up I scared one of the kids and they would cry. Then I had to sit up and rock them back to sleep. I felt like the night would never end.

The next morning I was exhausted. Looking around as the sun shined in the window and I put my hand up like that would block it from glaring in my eyes. My head was pounding from my fucked up sleep the night before. Between the bad dreams and feeding the baby every few hours I was beat. "Mommy, when is daddy coming. I want to play basketball," Keyon asked. I was not in the mood to hear shit about Kem so I just rubbed his back and stayed silent. One thing I never wanted to do was talk bad to my kids about their dad. But today was going to be a close one.

"Key lets go get breakfast," I told him as I slid off the king size bed. Keyon ran out of the room ahead of me. I felt myself slightly smile at his energy. Hell he needed to let me borrow some of it. Looking in the bassinet at Kaidence I stroked her silky jet black hair and she sighed in her sleep. My baby was so precious; she looked like a real life baby doll. Her pecan colored skin was like porcelain, every part of her was so delicate and perfect. I wished Kem would have been here to share these special moments but he chose not to be.

"Girl you can do this, I am going to get these kids together and take them with me for the day. Why don't you get some rest and start working on you." Inaya said as she grabbed Kaidence and began cooing at her. I don't know how she still loved babies with all the kids she had. Maybe the nanny helped. Shit I could use one of those. Naw who was I kidding I didn't like people in my space I was good taking care of my kids myself. I managed to pack the kids some toys, bottles and extra clothes even with my banging ass headache.

Walking into the kitchen Phantom was sitting at the island in my kitchen drinking something out of a coffee mug. I didn't buy coffee so I had no idea what the fuck it really was. He looked up at me and his face was so cold, like he was dead inside I felt a chill run through my body. I didn't know how the fuck Inaya slept next to this scary ass nigga. I nodded as a good morning because I felt like the cat had my tongue. Turning around I walked to the fridge to grab a bottle of water. I looked over my shoulder at this nigga a few times making sure he was still sitting down.

Hearing laugher I looked up to see Inaya giggling behind her hand. She walked up to Phantom and kissed him, running her hands over his braids. "Bae why you doing that shit to Nadège, she looking like she wants to run out of her own crib. Stop looking like the devil and shit, smile or something. Say good morning." She finished by mushing him in his head after he smirked her way. He looked different when he wasn't scowling. Iny really brought the best out in him. "Na don't even pay him any attention, he likes intimidating people with his mean looks. But he's like a teddy bear at heart."

Phantom stood up then and slapped her on the ass, hard. "Yo don't be fucking telling people I'm a teddy bear and shit. Unless Mister Teddy got an oozi in the trunk you got the wrong one. I'm going to handle business I will see you later." He handed her money even though I was sure she didn't need any. "Stay up Nadège, later," he said to me finally smiling slightly. For once his old mean ass looked human. Waving before he closed the door I rolled my eyes at Inaya.

"Girl your man looks like the fucking devil. I don't know what girls he was cheating on you with because personally I would be too scared to fuck him. He looks like one of those fuck you, choke you then kill you kind of dudes." Inaya was laughing again but I was serious. I guess there was some benefit to fucking with Satan; he could defend you in a fight. "Anyway what are you doing with my babies today," I asked. A part of me didn't really care I just wanted to get some sleep. I trusted Inaya and since Za'adore was being a bitch I really didn't have anyone else.

"We are going to visit Phantom's aunt, she moved back to Jersey because she was bored in Rochester. You need to sleep while I am gone. Once I drop these little monsters off we are going to take you to do something about those unibrow's you growing and the mop hairstyle you rocking. Be back soon," she called out walking to the door and giving me a princess wave. For the first time in a while the house was totally quiet. I made some tea, grabbed two Excedrin and made my way back to bed.

Before I knew it my cell phone alarm was going off and the time read two in the afternoon. Fuck I was in here sleeping like the dead. I checked for messaged but of course Kem was still letting me down, ignoring me and shit. I swore I had a wet dream about his ass while I was asleep. Sitting up and flinging the thick cream and pink comforter off of me I was happy my headache had left the building. I made my way to the shower and washed my body with some aromatherapy shit from Bath and Body works, this one was for stress relief. I could use some of that. I wanted to wash my hair but since I was going to the salon I decided to just wait.

"Come on slow poke, we are going to miss our appointment at the salon," fussed Inaya as she walked in my bedroom. She started picking out clothes for me to wear like she didn't see me sitting there with only a towel on. She walked to my dresser and started throwing clothes my way.

"Ok I am coming. Where are the kids?" I asked as I hurried and put on lotion and a baby blue bra and panty set.

"They are visiting Phantom's aunt for the day. You need the break and she loves kids. I will grab them later. Now let's go," she said clapping her hands. I guess I didn't have time for make-up but at least she let me slip into the tight ass black skinny jeans she picked for me and a white off the shoulder top. Hurrying to grab my purse and put on a pair of nude heels. Sliding into the soft leather seats of Inaya's rental I slid my shoes right back off and popped my feet up on the dashboard. "I am not you man so I need you to move those crusty toes off the dash. Especially because they need some work hunny."

Giving her the finger I picked up my phone to text Kem again but then I made a decision not to. I was going to have to be strong and start taking care of me. Not just financially, having money and a nice house and car were a blessing. But none of that shit meant anything if I drank stress for breakfast and Kem's nonsense for lunch. I refused to even look in another mirror until I got myself back to where I needed to be. Gripping the door I gave Inaya the side eye as she revved the engine on the Cayenne as she weaved in and out of traffic on the I80.

"You scared," she laughed? "You should see Phantom drive. I swear I almost pissed on myself the first time we took a road trip and he was pushing his Bentley over a hundred." Yup that was how she put up with mister crazy, she was misses crazy. We pulled up at the hair shop and like always a bunch of people where hanging outside doing nothing.

"Damn girl you sexy as fuck let me get your number," some short bald dude yelled as we walked by. Rolling my eyes I made sure he saw before I opened the door. I had no idea what I wanted to do to my hair so I told the girl to just pick a cute style. I felt like I was under the dryer forever but once I was done I fell in love with the red highlights she added to my hair. My curls where perfect and fell to both sides of my face with my part in the middle. Inaya got her short hair spiked and curled. She said she used to have long hair but honestly I couldn't picture her with it. The short styles really fit her.

Making our way next door to the nail shop I said a silent prayer that they didn't fuck up my feet. Looking around the place seemed nice, they had bright colors on the walls and framed images of nails everywhere. I was undecided on colors, I couldn't choose between the *fire engine red* and the *hottie tottie green*. The door opened and I could swear I smelled Kem's cologne. I guess I really couldn't get him off my mind. "Thanks Kem, see you later baby daddy," I heard someone call out.

Looking up I caught Kem handing Angalee two twenty dollar bills. His hand just stood there in mid-air like he didn't know what to do next. "Hey Kem, hope you're having a nice day. Oh the mortgage payment is due next week don't forget to make the payment." I smiled at both of them and gave a little wave even though I was crushed on the inside. I told myself I was done chasing Kemori and I meant it. I could tell by the slight smirk in his eyes he thought it was funny I told him to pay the mortgage on a house he bought me outright. I was just rubbing it in Angalee's face. She could suck, fuck or give Kem a hundred babies. I would always come first.

Before I could make my way to the massage chair Kem grabbed my arm. I hoped he didn't say shit to me, I didn't want to create a scene in front of all these people but I would. "Yo hold this ma," he said handing me a stack of money. "Your hair look good," he said and walked away. Angalee took her little forty dollars and sat at the table to get her nails done. I noticed she had a few broken ones. I bet Kem was just paying for her shit because he broke em. Side hoes killed me.

"You want to leave," Inaya asked me as I sat next to her.

"Girl hell no I earned this pedicure. Ask her if she wants to leave she is the one who over there looking sad. Shoving the money Kem gave me into my Louie bag I made a mental note to spend every fucking penny making myself feel better.

Standing up to pay I admired the neon green color I picked for my toes and nails. The nail lady, Michelle did her thing. My eye brows where once again perfectly arched and best of all I felt relaxed. "How much," I asked.

"It will be eighty five for hot stone pedicure, eyebrows and gel nails."

Pulling put a hundred dollar bills and three twenties I slid them across the counter. "I will cover her manicure as well. Keep the change."

"Why would you pay for my shit," Angalee wobbled after me to ask with an attitude. Looking at her average face and body bloated from pregnancy I was trying to figure out what Kem saw in her. He seemed addicted to her because he really couldn't leave her alone.

"I paid because I could," I said shrugging my shoulders. "My man gave me money, I didn't need charity. You know I am having his baby right." She flipped her raggedy ass twists so hard one of them swung around and flew in her eye. She acted like it didn't hurt but I I knew it did because her eye was watering.

"Angalee I know about the baby and guess what? I don't give a fuck. Now if you will excuse me I am going to the mall to shop with our man's money." Giving her the finger wave I let the door close in her face.

Chapter 4- Can't take this heart-break

Za'adore

Sophie had started going to pre-school so once Miss Peary went to the store I was in the house alone. After Avian played me the last time and chased me outside I began to give up on him. I thought we had something, a real love but his behavior lately had been outrageous. He was going hard in the streets and what time he didn't spend handling business he spent drinking and fucking other bitches. He has not come to one doctor's appointment with me to check on the baby and I was getting fed up. I had to take the bus to get to the doctor's appointment I had tomorrow because he never filed the insurance claim after Stacey Ann fucked up my car.

Sitting on the couch I turned on Judge Judy and began eating the pickles from the jar. I only had classes Tuesdays and Thursdays this semester so I didn't start until tomorrow. I was looking forward to getting out of the house because I felt like depression was setting in. But I was not looking forward to seeing Drue. He couldn't call me since I changed my number but he wouldn't stop sending me messages on social media. He was low key turning into a stalker.

Suddenly there was loud banging on the front door. Startled I spilled the pickle juice on my white tee. "Fuck," I mumbled. I guess Miss Peary forgot her key. Slowly I got up and walked into the front hall. The banging got louder. "Hold the fuck on," I screamed annoyed as hell. Flinging open the door I was surprised to see Nadège's friend Inaya standing there. She was gorgeous as always, well except the scowl she wore on her face. She had her arms crossed and was leaning against the door frame.

"Can I help you? How do you even know where the fuck I live?" I asked with an attitude. She wasn't the only one who could act like a bitch. She paused for a minute like she was thinking about a response. Her manicured hand tapped against her chin and her bright eyes slightly rolled upwards.

"Look Za'adore you really need to fix that attitude. Hell that's why you aint got nobody now. I came here to tell you that you need to call your friend. Make up with Na, apologize. She didn't deserve your attitude and she could use a friend right now." She said her little speech and waited for me to respond. I guess I was supposed to break into tears and confess how much I missed Na. Or thank her boujee ass driving all the way over here to tell me what I should be doing. Shaking my head I began closing the door in her face when I felt it being pushed back.

"Za'adore grow the fuck up," she said as she shoved past me and walked into the house. "I don't want to whoop your pregnant ass, but I will. Come sit down, offer me a drink or some shit so we can figure this out. I came here to do something and I am not leaving until it's done." She slid her feet out of her slip on black and white checkered Vans and went to sit on my couch. Before I could process what was going on she had changed the channel to some House Hunters show and was eating one of my pickles.

I honestly didn't know if I should laugh or cry. Maybe she wasn't boujee maybe she was just crazy. Her arrogance was kind of amusing. I slowly wandered over to the loveseat across from her and sat down. I was tired of emotionally waring with everyone. Maybe I should just listen to what she had to say. "Well you made yourself at home so go on and talk. Maybe I have shit to do." I said, still with an attitude.

"I know you think I am the enemy that I came into the picture and stole your best friend. But I'm not, I met Nadège and she became like a little sister to me. That doesn't mean you lost your place in her life. Hell Na misses you, I know she does. I have no idea what you got going on in your life but I can see by the look in your eyes you going through some shit. Dealing with these nigga's will stress you out if you let them. You probably looking at me like I got it all, thinking I aint never been through shit. I been through a lot and then some, even had my daughter kidnapped by her abusive father. Za'adore we can start over. We can be friends and you and Nadège can get your friendship back."

"Inaya I am sorry about your daughter, you damn right I couldn't imagine you going through anything. Hell you look like one of those African Princesses and act like you have the perfect life. I don't know where me and Na started to lose our closeness. I guess it was my fault, when I lost my first baby and Avian wasn't all I thought he was I felt jealous. Her and Kem situation was crazy but I could tell he really loved her. I wish I had that kind of love. Then Na didn't have time for me and started keeping secrets. Everything just changed and fast, it was hard on me. I am sorry though, I was a horrible friend to Nadège. I guess all I am going through now waiss my karma." I began crying and Inaya came to sit next to me and give me a hug. She really wasn't that bad. I just never gave her a chance.

We sat and talked for a few hours. We even ordered some Chinese food. Avian's baby was greedy as fuck and I had to eat something every few hours or I would get nauseous. Licking the sauce from the orange chicken off my lips I sat back and smiled. "I still remember when I first met Nadège. She moved in the building next door to me when she was seven and I was five. I thought she had the best life because her mom used to be home every day. Cooking and taking care of her, I never had that. But once her brother's died and her father left things changed. We were both fucked up. Her mom started popping pills and drinking. Her mom started treating Nadège like she killed her brothers or something. Even with all her own shit at home Na always looked out for me, she used to make sure we both ate when our parents just didn't give a damn."

"I still remember the first time she gave me a perm. Neither one of us knew what the hell we was doing. She was like it's some directions on this box so we just going to read em. She left that perm in my head so long I had a whole bald spot in the middle. We had to steal sulfur eight from the Duane Reid so I could grow my shit back. I miss my friend. I just don't think she will forgive me."

"Listen, just call her. You and Na have a lot of history. Stuff like that just can't be erased with a few angry words and a fucked up attitude. Just fix your attitude. Don't let Avian change you, hell Kem either. However he treats Nadège that's not you, it's not your business. Be her best friend and let the rest go. I am about to get out of here because I am headed home today. I miss my kids. Make sure you call her up and next time you see me have a smile, a hug, I will even take a sandwich shit." Inaya reached over and rubbed my belly and then gave me a hug.

As I walked her to the door Avian was coming in from God knows where. I swear his whole attitude lately has changed. It was like a man I didn't even know. He still spent time with Sophie but acted like I didn't exist. He wouldn't fuck me, speak to me and just looked past me when I was around. I could smell the liquor on his breath before he was even in my space.

"Yea baby keep that pussy wet for daddy. I will be there soon I just have some business to handle first." He spoke into his phone with a big ass drunk smile on his face. "Hey babe I am going to call you back when I am on my way I see my homeboy's wife." He hung up and gave Inaya a friendly hug. "Hey girl, where Phantom crazy ass at?," he asked acting like he didn't just walk through the door talking to some other bitch.

"So who the fuck was that on your phone Avian," I said in the rudest tone I could find. I was ready to go to the kitchen and grab the nearest item that I could use for a weapon. This nigga had me twisted. I could see that Inaya was keeping a straight face and I respected her for that. I was embarrassed already and didn't feel like pity from her pretty ass.

"Hell Za I don't know the bitch name, Sarah, Suzette, Saran something with an S. All I know is she got good pussy and gives even better head. Now move the fuck out my way I got shit to do." He shoved past me almost hitting my belly. Avian has turned into a different kind of asshole. I finished walking my company out the door and went back to the couch. After sitting there for a while I began thinking of ways to get back at Avian.

Hearing the front door Sophie walked in with Miss Peary behind her. "Mama, I want to go watch my new movie I got at the store." She hugged me then began jumping up and down holding a new DVD. The colorful animals held microphones and the title was Sing. Oh boy, I remember taking her to see it in the movies and she made us take her three times in a week. The joys of mother hood I guess. At least Sophie still loved me. She was always on my side. She had started calling me mom about four months ago and I never stopped her. Surprisingly neither did Avian.

"Ok baby, I made you a snack of celery and cream cheese on the table with your favorite juice. After you wash your hands you can have a snack and then watch your movie. Mommy is going to lie down a little so be good for Miss Peary." Avian made his way downstairs and picked up Sophie. Thank God he smelled like cologne and mouth wash instead of weed and liquor.

I wandered off to let them have some alone time. I went to the guest room and sank down on the bed. All of my stuff was now in this room. I moved out of Avian's room and he never asked me back. I waited up a lot of nights hoping he would come in here and tell me he missed me or apologize for how he had been acting. I picked up the framed picture of me, Na and Keyon at Dave and Busters a few years ago. It was all I had from my past life. No baby pictures or child hood memories. I could pack all of my stuff in a few suitcases and that would be it.

I thought about what Inaya said and decided to reach out to Nadège. I was going to call but after dialing the number three different times I never pressed send. I decided a text would be better. That way if she had an attitude I wouldn't hear it in her voice.

Me: *Na I wanted to apologize for everything. I have been terrible to you and you didn't deserve that. I was jealous of you and Kem's relationship and I turned into the worst type of friend, an enemy. I pray you can forgive me because I miss my best friend and I never meant to hurt you. I hope you and the kids are doing well and I cannot wait to meet baby Kaidence.*

I pressed send and watched as the blue bar across the top of the phone slid all the way across and then disappeared letting me know the message went through. There was no changing my mind now. I heard Avi come upstairs with Sophia and tell her to get ready for bed and he would watch a little of her movie. I made a decision in that moment. I was tired of Avian acting like I wasn't there. I didn't ask to be a part of his life and now that I was he treated me like a fucking inconvenience.

I hurried and took a shower because I needed to be done before Avian went to see his new "babe". As soon as I got out I used regular Vaseline lotion and didn't put on any perfume. I was not letting Avian know what was up and my perfume would have given me away. I put on a light grey sweat suit from the GAP and a pair of white Reebok classics. Cracking the bedroom door open I walked quietly down the stairs and right out the front door. I knew he was taking the Audi tonight because his drinking and driving caught up to him and he crashed the Benz last week.

I crept to the back of the Audi and popped the trunk. I tried to gracefully lower myself into the trunk but ended up rolling in instead. I quickly lowered the trunk using the child safety latch. I must have been out there a while because I fell asleep. I was lucky I didn't suffocate or some shit. Maybe I watched too many movies. Finally the car came to life and Avian began driving. He went so fast and it felt like he hit every fucking bump in the world. I definitely didn't think this shit through all the way.

About an hour later the deafening music finally got quiet and the car rolled to a stop. I heard him talking to someone outside of the car.

"Baby I told you I was coming to check on ya'll. Why you standing out here in this tiny ass outfit, you going to freeze my shorty." I heard a female say something in response but it was too low for me to catch what she said. I cracked the trunk by releasing the child safety latch. I peeked out to see Avian rubbing a girls belly and holding her close. The girl was not ugly at all. She was darker than me, maybe caramel with her hair in a cute ponytail with a hump in the front. Her body was pretty slim except the small round belly in front of her. So this was Lena.

All this time Avian played me, if this was the case he should have just been with this bitch. Hell he knew her before me. I couldn't watch anymore. I let the trunk fly open and I climbed out. I made sure to grab the tire iron that was lying in the back with me on my way. "Avian what the hell," she screamed as she saw me.

I made sure to charge at both of them swinging like a crazy person. I could hear someone's bones crunching but I didn't take the time to check on whose. Lena was on the ground clutching her belly with tears rolling down her cheek. "Za'adore STOP she is pregnant. What the fuck is your problem. Are you smoking or something?" Avian shouted trying to grab me and not get bust upside the head.

"Oh so now you give a fuck if someone's pregnant? I guess this baby matters to you while neither one of ours did. Well Avian Evans you want to know what is wrong with me. Not a damn thing. I am finally ok. I am able to see clearly now. You didn't love me, never gave a fuck about me just wanted to make a fool of me." I went to hit him in his leg but he grabbed my arm and twisted it behind my back. The tire iron dropped to the ground with a clang and next thing I know I felt my arms being restrained.

"Bitch you killed our baby," Lena yelled as she ran behind me. Avian moved me to the back of him and grabbed her by the throat.

"Lena, stay the fuck in your place. I know she fucked you up ma and I am sorry for that. But don't you ever lift your hand up to my shorty especially when she carrying my seed. Take yo ass in the house and clean up. If you need to see a doctor Uber to the hospital and call me when you know what's up." Avian took a rope out of his backseat after he dismissed her ass.

I looked at him with confusion. I was hurt that he did this, shit that he cheated on me to begin with. That another woman was carrying his baby, something that was a part of him. But I felt good that he stood up for me. I didn't want to feel good but I couldn't help it. I craved his love, any kindness from him. I eyed him wondering what the fuck he was about to do with that rope. He walked towards me without hesitation. I could see the fire in his eyes. I guess I pushed him too far for real this time. He grabbed my wrists and tied both of my hands together.

The trunk was still opened from when I climbed out. He gently picked me up and shoved me in the trunk. "Since you like riding in the trunks sit yo retarded ass back there and think about the stupid shit you be doing," he said before he slammed the trunk closed. I was left in the darkness with my hands tied in front of me. I couldn't move and this baby was sitting on my bladder. I swear Avian took the longest route from the Bronx back to Long Island. After what seemed like forever we pulled up home. I could hear the garage door open as he pulled the car in. I guess he didn't want to have the neighbors see him pulling a tied up girl out of the trunk. These people probably think we crazy over here already.

Avian let me out but kept my ass tied up like a prisoner of war. He didn't say anything to me but mumbled a lot under his breath. As soon as we got to the guest room he flung open the door so hard I knew the whole house heard the bang. Pulling off the rope he ran his hands up and down my body. Stopping at my swollen belly the baby kicked and he spread his fingers wider. A smile touched his face until he looked up and caught my eye.

"I am leaving stay your ass in this house unless you going to school or doing something useful. I am sorry I was ever stuck with yo ass. I used to think that Charmayne and Alicia were a thorn in my side. You are the whole thorn tree. You made them seem like angels. I am walking away from you right now because I am trying my best to hold on to my temper. To not fuck you up pregnant or not. Za I used to love you. I gave up everything for you. I had to turn my back on my family, my pops for your ass. You broke my heart and I just can't forgive that."

He said the last part low, like he was trying to convince himself and not me. It had been a while but I knew the tears where coming. This finally felt like the end. I knew I had to figure out a plan B because I could tell Avian was at the end of his rope with me. His heart had turned cold and it was my fault. I only talked to Drue because I wasn't woman enough to figure out how to handle relationship issues. Lying on my side I grabbed my pillow and cried myself to sleep.

Chapter 5- The good, the bad and the new Kemori

Riding through the streets I stopped at the bar on Grant to get a drink. I knew the drinking and smoking been getting out of control lately. Not being with the girl I love has been getting to me. I was also dealing with Avian and his shit. He went from a pussy to a damn killer. He murdered ten people just last week who he thought were stealing from the fam. I still couldn't believe he knocked off Charmayne funky ass and Za'adore's mother. I aint mad at him for that but his wild ass behavior was starting to stress me out.

"Yo give me three shots of Patron." I yelled to the waitress who kept throwing lustful looks my way. She was aright, big breasts spilling out of her skimpy black shirt and a fat ass stuffed into some painted on blue jeans. Her short bob was classy and framed her cute face. Maybe I would get into that a little later. I hadn't seen my kids in a few weeks because I been trying to avoid Nadège's ass plus I was back and forth to Atlanta meeting one of my connects. Sending a text I asked could I see the kids the next day. I downed my three drinks and enjoyed the burn in the back of my throat. Nadège still didn't respond to my message, she left me right on read. Fuck her.

"Yo ma, what time you getting off tonight," I asked waving her over.

"I am ready now if you are," she said using her pink tongue to lick her lips. I noticed she had a double tongue ring in her mouth and that shit made me rock up. I couldn't wait to see what that mouth could do. Throwing down a few fifties I got up motioning for her to follow me. Once we made it to the car I hit the unlock button and hopped in. As soon as my ass hit the seat I was undoing my belt buckle and pulling my dick out.

"Damn nigga straight like that huh? I thought you was trying to get to know me or hold a conversation." She said screwing up her face and fake sounding confused.

"Come on bih you knew the deal when you came out here. Don't blow my fucking high. The only fucking conversation I was interested in was your mouth talking to my dick." Grabbing shorty by the back of her neck I guided her head closer to my man. She snaked out her tongue and teased the head just like a pro. Her hot saliva was dripping all over my wood and her hands where everywhere, stroking and caressing. "Yes girl give me that real sloppy head. I want to see you with that cum all over your face." I coached her to keep going. I pushed her head down further forcing myself to the back of her throat.

I could tell by the way she was moaning she was enjoying sucking me off just as much as I was. Her moans turned me on even more. I was so into what she was doing I didn't care that we were on a busy street in my car. I didn't have to feel guilty about cheating on Nadège because that was a wrap. I was free to do whatever I wanted whenever I wanted. Shorty started spitting on my dick then slurping it back up. "Shit ma just like that," I couldn't hold back if I wanted to. My cum erupted and I bust all over her face and hair.

"Damn nigga you are so fucking rude. The rumors about yo ass was true you are disrespectful." She bitched while licking the thick white cum from her lips. I was disrespectful but she was out here in a car licking up my sperm like ice cream. I threw her ass some tissues and reached over her to open the door. She didn't say shit else just slid around and hopped out the ride. I reached in my pocket to throw lil mama a few bills for her trouble but all my hand caught was air.

What the fuck. I knew I had a knot of cash in my front right pocket. Getting out of the car and standing up I searched both pockets. Looking up at the girl from the bar I noticed her trying to wave a taxi down. Running over I grabbed her by the neck as soon as one pulled up. "Bitch you want to rob me," I yelled tossing her ass to the ground.

"Sir, sir, leave the young lady alone." The Taxi driver hopped out, his accent was thick and his turban was tilting as he tried to hop around the fender to get to us.

"Hey if you know what's good for you son just get in the car and pull the fuck off." He still stood there watching me kick shorty in the ribs. I wasn't trying to fuck her up, I was pissy drunk so holding on to any control was a challenge. Seeing this dude was going to be a hard ass I took my gun out and shot in the air. That sent him running for his Taxi. He hopped in so fast he almost slid back out on those wooden beads he had for a cushion.

I started to feel sick from all the drinks I had in the past twenty four hours. Leaning against the light post I put my head down for a second. Wham, I felt something hard hit me in the head. This bitch was fighting me. How the fuck you rob me and then try and come for me. That blow to the head woke me the fuck up. Turning around fast I grabbed her by her throat. "Bitch give me my fucking bread." I shook her hoe ass like a rag doll. Snatching the purse she was carrying I looked inside to see my money right on top.

Dropping her and the bag I pocketed my shit and walked back to my car. I can't believe a bitch caught me slipping like that. I needed to get my head right. Calling Nadège a few times I was going to keep calling until her ass answered. "Kem, do you fucking know what time it is," she finally picked up and said in an annoyed tone.

"Yo I don't give a fuck about the time. I was robbed, set up. All you bitches are the same. This shit was your fault. If I never met you this wouldn't be happening to me. I would be focused. Instead I am in these streets slipping. Na why, why did you do this to me," I asked while leaning my head back on the leather seats?

"Kemori you sound like you are drunk and what the fuck you mean you was robbed? Are you ok? Maybe you need to go sleep it off." She was concerned but seemed annoyed at the same time. I guess me waking her up was not helping this shit.

"I miss my kids Na, I need to see my kids. Imma pick them up tomorrow. I know you won't keep them away from me. You're not like that, you're not a bitch." I didn't even know what the fuck I was saying I was so fucked up. Reaching into the middle console I reached for the blunt I knew I had there. I listened to Nadège try to calm me down. I guess she thought that shit was working but her talking to me like a kid was pissing me off. Inhaling the Kush I felt my body relax and my mind go blank. This was one of the reasons I never had a fucking problem killing people. Good weed can cure anything.

I decided I needed to end the call before I started telling Nadège I missed and loved her. I couldn't keep going back down that road. It never led to good things for me or her. "Na I just want to spend time with my kids tomorrow. I don't need a lecture or a talking too. I just need you to have my kids ready when I get there."

"Kem, we are not home. We are out of town. When we get back you can see them."

"Out of town doing fucking what, I don't remember you asking me to go out of town," I shouted into the phone. Now I was pissed this shit right here was what I was talking about. "Na, you think you could just take my kids and don't say a fucking word. Kaidence is not even old enough to be traveling."

"Kem if you weren't being such an asshole I would tell you where we are or would have let you know I was leaving. I am tired of you thinking you run me. We have kids together that is all. I am not a car that you ride when you feel like it and keep me parked in the garage when you are bored. Now when I get home I will let you know so you can see your kids. Don't call me Kem I will call you," she said clicking off her phone and giving me the dial tone.

"Fuck," I yelled as I banged the dashboard. I knew I could have called Phantom to have him get a location from his wife. But fuck it I shouldn't have to so that shit to find out where my kids where. Starting up the car I thought about going to Angalee's crib but decided one miserable baby moms was enough for the night.

Nadège

Looking down at the phone I scrolled to Kem's name and added his ignorant ass to the block list. I would deal with him once I got home. Scrolling through my messages was when I noticed the text from Za'adore. I left it sitting there unread for a few days. I finally clicked on it and looked at her apology. I closed my eyes, I was exhausted. It was a long drive from Jersey to Rochester, especially with two little kids. After Kem packed his shit I decided to come and visit Inaya and Azia. I needed a change of scenery and it was quiet down here.

I wasn't sure how to respond to Za'adore. I wanted to just say fuck her but it was hard to let go of a friendship that we had for so long. I sent a response telling her we should have lunch when I got back in town. Crazy I was just doing so many things on my own. There was a time when Za'adore always knew what I was up to. Flinging Keyon's feet off of me I rolled over to try and go back to sleep.

Waking up the next morning to a crying Kaidence and Keyon jumping on the bed meant it was going to be a busy day. I was up for hours after I decided to go to bed. Wondering who robbed Kem and if he was ok. I guess getting over him and doing me was still a work in progress.

The next day when I finally woke up for real I felt free. No more Kem or Sam or any stress for the moment. I fed the kids and took a shower. We were going to a museum for kids than me and the girls were going out later on. I put a little make up and lip gloss on before bumping my curls. Looking in the mirror I loved the way the light wash ripped capris fit me. I had a white crop top that had black lace around the top. I slid my feet into a pair of black sandals with a suede bow on top.

"Shit you down here trying to cheat on my boy or what?" Phantom asked when I walked downstairs.

"Yea ok," I said rolling my eyes. I guess Phantom ass didn't scare me much anymore. I was getting used to him. The girls all wandered in along with all their kids. There were a lot of kids. All of us piled into two trucks and were on our way.

****

Leaning back in the plane I took another sip of the red wine and prepared for take-off. I was flying home since I didn't drive myself down. Luckily Rochester was only an hour flight to JFK. I had so much fun with Inaya and Azia I didn't want to leave but I knew if I kept the kids away from Kem much longer he would be coming to find my ass. I had him on the block list for a week but I think Phantom snitched and told him were I was because that was his boy.

I fell asleep and what seemed like a few minutes later we were fastening our seatbelts to land. Both kids were still sleeping luckily. After waiting twenty minutes for my luggage and even longer for an Uber we finally made it home. I walked in hoping to see Kem but he wasn't there. "Come on kids let's unpack then we can have lunch."

I finally unblocked Kem and told him he could see his kids. He must have been parked around the fucking corner because he was walking through the front door not long after. "Kemori, you don't live here anymore so please knock on the damn door." I demanded in a cold tone. I was annoyed he really left me and just walked in my house looking like a million bucks. He was wearing pair of red shorts a white Armani shirt and some white Armani sneakers. His platinum grill, iced out bracelet and chain were blinding in the sun light. I wondered what bitch he had braiding his hair because those looked fresh.

"What the fuck you looking at Na, something you can't have anymore." He said talking shit. He went in the fridge and started taking out baby bottles filled with my breast milk.

"Shit you mean something I don't want anymore," I shot back.

"Yo I will bring them back later. Don't call me about them either. They coming home when the fuck I bring them since you just dipped with my kids for over a week." I just shrugged and went upstairs to tell Keyon goodbye. I have been dragging the past few days so sleep was going to be my best friend.

Chapter 6- Your time is up

Za'adore

I woke up feeling stiff as hell and hungry. I forgot to eat last night and now my stomach was growling and the baby was kicking the shit out of me. I had a doctor's appointment after school to figure out the sex of the baby and I hoped Avian showed up, but doubted he would. Miss Peary was so sweet, she made me my favorite pancakes with strawberries for breakfast and left them on the table. After eating I waddled back up-stairs and picked out some clothes to wear. I settled on a navy blue tights and a black hoodie with red and blue writing. I managed to put my hair into a slicked back bun and put on some red Air Maxes.

I grabbed my book bag and ordered an Uber to take me to school. I still had some money from when Avian used to fuck wit me and that was how I was surviving but the money was quickly dwindling to nothing. If I wasn't pregnant I would be taking the bus but this baby was kicking my ass. Walking into the college I pulled out the paper with my schedule. Seeing my first class was Sociology 101 I walked slowly down the hallway. I was praying to not see Drue. I had not spoken to him since I changed my phone number. I didn't want to get caught up in a dude that I didn't love. He was just someone to pass the time when Avian used to ignore me. I made it through the first two classes with no Drue. Just when I felt like I could avoid him he strolled into my final class of the day. It was Linguistics and sadly one I couldn't transfer out of.

"Wow, I guess I see now why you began ignoring me and shit. I was going to tell your man about us but I heard in the streets he found out on his own. Remember I told you not to fuck with me. You should have been left you. He really got you out here looking like a baby mamma. Hair gelled back, tights and a hoodie on. Where your big ass hoop earrings at?" He mocked me as he slid into the seat next to mine.

We still had five minutes before the class started and I wished he would just go the fuck away. He was not someone I was interested in speaking to right now or ever. Even though Drue used to say all the right things there was always something about him that got under my skin. "Drue can we just pretend we never met? I mean I have my situation," I said motioning to my pregnant belly. "And I am sure you have yours."

"Yea whatever B. Sorry I ever started liking your fake ass. Told me all that shit about how you was done with this nigga Avi, how he was more of a captor and not a man. Now you and him living happily ever after." With that he turned his head to his laptop that was in front of him and didn't say anything else.

I tried my hardest to pay attention to the different sounds the teacher was pointing out for each region of the US, but it was hard to concentrate. I kept checking my phone to see if Avian responded about coming to the baby's ultrasound. He didn't. The doctor's office was in walking distance but for August it was kind of chilly outside. I guess I would have to just suck it up. Tears came to my eyes as I thought about what Drue said. *Living happily ever after, I wish, I thought to myself.* More like living with a man I love but who hates me. I had no one and nothing with a baby on the way.

The only good thing that happened today was receiving a message from Nadège asking to meet for lunch. I knew it didn't mean she accepted my apology but it was a place to start. As the professor said class dismissed I was already out of my seat and halfway to the door. Walking outside it had started to drizzle outside. "Great," I murmured under my breath. Throwing the hood over my hair so it didn't frizz up I started walking. Once I reached the corner Drue pulled up in his all black Honda Accord.

"Yo you need a ride or something? A girl in your condition shouldn't be out here walking in the rain." He gave me a lopsided smile as he tilted his head. Drue was not ugly at all, he just had boyish looks. His soft curly hair was cut short and his Hershey colored skin looked good against his red shirt. He even had one dimple when he smiled. The only manly looking thing was his muscles that I couldn't view since he was in the car. But compared to Avian he looked like a toddler. I giggled out loud as I thought of strapping him into a booster seat like I did Sophie.

Damn I missed having my own car. The slight drizzle was beginning to turn into a down pour. I checked my phone one last time silently praying that Avian had responded to me. Seeing no new messages I decided to just take the ride. Fuck it, if Avian wanted to leave me and his baby for dead fuck him. I was getting fed up. The ride to the OBGYN was a silent one. For that I was thankful. I had a lot on my mind anyway.

I was surprised when Drue parked the car and began getting out. "Umm Drue where you think you going," I asked with an attitude? He didn't respond just slammed the door and followed me to the door. I didn't ask this mother fucker to accompany me anywhere. Looking at the time on my phone I didn't have time to argue I was about to be late.

"Two o'clock appointment for Za'adore Stevens with Doctor Yan," I said when I got to the receptionist.

'Have a seat and someone will be with you soon." I was starting to feel sad that Avian would really let me go through this alone. It was a blessing that this baby made it so far considering what happened to the last one.

"So you want a boy or a girl," Drue asked with a smile, like it was his baby or something. I just shrugged and focused on the Parent magazine I was reading. The baby strollers with the bassinets on them looked so cute but the cost on one was insane. Who paid over a thousand dollars for a stroller? Reality TV stars I guess.

"Za'adore Stevens," the nurse called out. She stood there holding her little clipboard smiling. The staff here was friendly, and mostly white people came here. I was glad so I wouldn't be here running into Avian's pop offs and shit.

"Drue I am good I can go in by myself." I said as he followed me to the back.

"Nah I want to glimpse that fat ass pussy anyway I can since you was acting stingy with a nigga before." I rolled my eyes at his retarded ass. It was an ultrasound not a vaginal exam. Once I laid on the table the technician walked in and started by tucking a towel in the top of my tights.

"Is this the father," she asked me looking at Drue.

"Fuck no that's not the father, I am," Avian said walking through the door. If looks could kill both me and Drue would be dead. "Son good looking out giving my shorty a ride and all but we got it from here." He said damn near knocking Drue off the chair.

Drue got up, giving Aviana dirty look in the process. "Aright Za holla at me later if you need me," he said before walking out the door. Avian sat next to me and grabbed my hand. His grip was tight as hell. I tried to remove it but he slit his eyes and stared up at me. The tech was rambling on and on about what she would be checking for and how sometimes we could not tell the sex of the baby because the legs would be closed. I could tell by the nods Avian was giving her he was just keeping a calm front so he wouldn't cause a scene.

"Ok you will feel a cold sensation as I put the gel on. Sorry about that," she said as she squirted the blue stuff on my belly. I was so nervous about being caught here with Drue. I knew I should have fought harder for him to drop me off and go. God alone knew what Avian was going to do to me when we left this appointment. I could feel my stomach twist into knots and I felt like I couldn't breathe. "Ma'am your blood pressure is way up and your baby has balled up into a corner in your uterus. Are you experiencing any pain or discomfort?" The tech had a concerned look on her face.

"I am fine, can we please move forward with the exam I am probably just hungry." I lied. I was scared, the pain was in my heart and the stress was in my head.

"Ok well I am going to step out and speak to the doctor. Please excuse me for a moment." She walked out of the room leaving me and Avi alone.

"Yo, you need to fucking relax so I can see my baby. I came here for my kid not you. I don't have shit to say to you and don't worry I am not going to fuck you up while you carrying my shorty. I am just going to continue not fucking with you because I don't wife hoes. To think Za'adore I was going to wife your lying cheating ass." He laughed at himself and began texting on his phone.

I felt a few tears slide down my face. I couldn't even be mad because I did this. I did lie and technically I cheated on him. Today was the dumbest shit I ever did. I tried to slow my breathing down as I wiped away the tears. I knew the doctor would be worried and I didn't need these people in my business. Doctor Yan walked in the room with her stark white lab coat on. She began sliding the wand over my belly and clicking the computer to take pictures I guess. It looked like the baby was relaxed now. I could see feet and legs and hear the heartbeat.

Avian sat forward like he was very interested. At least he loved his kid. "Do you want to know the sex of the baby," Doctor Yan asked? We both shook our head yes. "Ok so it looks like you will be having a little boy," she said. Avian's face lit up like a kid on Christmas. Looks like he always wanted a boy. The doctor wiped off my belly and handed us each some photos. "Za'adore with your history and your age I am extremely worried about your blood pressure being so high. I need you to make sure you are eating right for the baby and avoid stress."

"Thank you doctor I will," I responded while getting up to go.

Avian

Getting up from the chair in the exam room I wanted to pat myself on the back for not fucking up Za'adore for her dumb shit. She really had another nigga in the room with her chilling like I didn't even exist. I was really lost on how to handle this shit. I never had any female running circles around me but this one was pushing all my buttons. Walking outside I noticed Za wasn't behind me. What the fuck game was she playing now?

Looking around I noticed her walking away. She had her head down I guess to avoid the rain and her hoodie pulled up. "Yo what the hell are you doing," I asked? She didn't even look up or stop. I jumped in my car and pulled up next to her. "Za get in the fucking car." I yelled causing her to jump startled.

She just shook her head, looking at me with her big sad eyes. We stared at each other a few seconds before she started walking again. Fuck it, if she wanted to walk in the rain let her, if something happens to my son because of her stupidity that was her ass. I peeled off making sure to hit a puddle and splash her ass as I drove away. Fucking dummy was pissing me the hell off.

As soon as I made it in the house I bust into the guest room where Za was sleeping. I pulled her luggage out of the closet and started packing all her shit. I mean hell she wanted to be with that baby looking ass nigga Drue so let her. An hour passed and she still had not made it to the house. I was just about to call her when I heard the door open downstairs. She walked into the room soaking wet. I guess her hard headed ass walked the whole way home.

"What the hell are you doing in my room," she asked in an outraged voice. She began stripping out of her wet clothes when he eyes fell on the luggage I had packed next to the bed.

"Look I am done with you. Tomorrow get your shit and get out. Honestly I don't give a fuck where you go or what you do. I told you stop playing games with me but your trick ass couldn't stay away from baby boy so go live with him." I turned to walk away but stopped when she walked up to me and punched me in the face.

"Avian I will leave this house right now. It's not a problem. I trusted you. You promised to take care of me and treat me good but instead you kick me and our baby in the streets. You knew I had nothing, crazy ass Stacey Ann ruined my car. You stopped giving me money even though we were having a baby. Do you know how many days I couldn't even eat at school because I had nothing. I bet you cannot understand how hard it was for a pregnant person to wait all day for food. What did you expect me to do? Keep allowing you to treat me like shit? Walk to the doctors in the pouring rain after I called you a hundred times? I have been there for you. I gave you all of my love and all you did was cheat on me and mistreat me. You never even apologized for getting Lena ass pregnant. So yea I was wrong to talk to Drue but you were wrong too."

She threw her wet clothes in the hamper and opened up her bag to find something dry. Before I could really process what she said or how hurt she was Za 'adore had grabbed her bags and headed downstairs. I thought she was gone but an hour later when I went to check on Sophie I found her on the floor next to her bed. She was curled up in the fetal position with her hand holding on to Sophie's. I could still see the tears in her eyes from crying. Damn, she really loved my daughter and I couldn't even find it in my heart to forgive her. I knew she wasn't really fucking wit the nigga Drue, just talking to him and sending those pictures. If I was honest I drove her to it.

I reached down and picked her up, carrying her back down the hall I took her into my room and laid her on the bed. Removing her shoes and pants she snuggled into the down comforter and let out a snore. I figured her pregnancy was making her ass tired. I got in bed with her and rubbed on her belly. I could lightly feel my son kick. I wasn't no better than my pops. I wasn't doing right by my boy at all. Pulling Za close held her in my arms until I finally fell asleep.

The next morning I woke up with a smile on my face. Until I looked at the side Za'adore was on and realized she was gone.

Chapter 7 – I keep trying to love you
Nadège

I walked past Planned Parenthood for the fifth time with tears falling down my face. Shit it seems like all I have done for the past year is cry and cry some more. I didn't tell anyone I was pregnant not even Inaya and she was like my sister. I have spent the past week talking myself into this abortion and right back out. I refused to speak to this baby like I did my other kids when I found out I was pregnant. Even though my living situation was stable and money was no longer a problem physically I didn't think I could manage another small child alone. And alone was what I was.

It was like the moment Kem's father was murdered it changed him. Even though we were on the outs I tried my hardest to be there for him but he just pushed me further away. Kem picks up the kids on Wednesdays and every other weekend. Money was deposited in my account weekly and I was ignored otherwise. I had a toddler, a six month old baby and now I was five weeks pregnant. This could not be life. I just started getting my life together, going to school and thinking about opening an online boutique.

Feeling the light drizzle turn into a downpour I took that as a sign to head inside the glass door with blue letters. I knew this was wrong but I also knew having another baby and not being able to pay it attention was also wrong. I didn't want to hate my kids because I was overwhelmed or stressed. Hell Kem probably didn't even want this baby since he had one on the way with his bitch, I heard she was due any day now. I am sure he ran over there to her once he left our house, left me. Then my mind thought back to the car accident and the rape, Sam was still out there and I couldn't put another child at risk.

As soon as I finally began the walk towards the receptionist desk I felt someone grab my wrist so hard I thought it would snap.

"So this is the shit you up too, out here killing my kid without saying a fucking word to anyone huh. Well that shit aint happening today, now let's go," Kemori said while dragging me back towards the front doors.

"Sir, what you are doing is wrong, she has a right to do whatever she would like with her body and I will call the police if I have to." The receptionist yelled to him as he continued to pull me towards the door. My arm felt like it was going to be ripped from the socket at any moment. I was shocked because Kem was never really violent towards me.

"Hey bitch mind your fucking business and call the cops if you want this is my girl and what I say goes. If you weren't so blind you would see that she doesn't want this, look at the way she was crying and shit." The tone of his voice got louder and louder and so did his grip. Deciding to get him out of there before my children's father ended up in prison I walked in the direction of the door this time I was almost pulling him since he had stopped to curse out the old ass white lady with the wire rimmed glasses.

As soon as we made it outside he slammed his fists into the brick building. I knew he was mad at me, hell I was mad at me but I didn't know what else to do. I felt like my back was against the wall. "Nadège why? I mean ma am I that fucking terrible you would rather kill a nigga baby than have a piece of me growing inside you? I was mad when you thought about aborting Kaidence, even if it was only for a second that you questioned yourself. I was still pissed but at least I understood. I get it when you were broke, living in the streets with Keyon and scared. But that shit doesn't even fucking apply right now, I made sure yo ass has everything. You don't work, you got the big house the new car. I get up every day and risk my soul in these streets so you and they could live comfortable. Even though we not together ma I never put you last. You and my sorties are always first. I spend time with them on the regular. But the thought of another baby with me makes you want to have an abortion?"

I felt my heart break again, this must make the thousandth time since I have met Kemori. Only this time it broke because I just realized the pain I caused him. I was selfish trying to kill our baby. Shit I didn't even let him know what was up. I mean yea I tried but I could have waited. Kem has been a great father if nothing else. I could tell he wasn't even made. He was hurt. He stood there with the veins popping out of his neck and tears in his eyes. His hands where clenched at his sides.

Walking up to him I wrapped my arms around his waist and laid my head on his chest. "Kemori I am sorry. I didn't want to hurt you, hell I really didn't want to hurt our baby. I was afraid to have all these small kids and raise them alone. We are not together and even though you're a great dad I need the support of a partner. Kem I will figure it out. I will keep our baby. I still love you Kem," I whispered the last part.

I thought he was going to push me away, or hell throw me to the ground and step on my little ass. Instead he pulled me close. We stood outside the Planned Parenthood just like that. The rain lightly falling and making our clothes wet. He rested his face on the top of my head and sighed. "Na I am trying to understand. I really am. Let's go get you some food. You want IHOP." Thinking about pancakes and bacon I smiled and nodded my head. I took a few more minutes to inhale his Gucci Guilty cologne. No man could ever replace Kem in my life.

I left my car and rode in the BMW with Kem. Kicking off my flats I propped my feet on the dashboard, turned the heat on the seat and rested my eyes. It had been a long twenty four hours, dealing with all those emotions sucked the life out of me. We made it to the IHOP and parked. Kem even opened the doors for me when we walked in. Funny how we got along better now that we were not trying to be together anymore, I guess just being friends was the key.

I sat down and ordered a stack of blueberry pancakes, scrambled eggs and double bacon. Kemori got a hot chocolate and a steak and eggs. "Kem I wanted to go back to school in a few weeks but with another baby coming that is on hold again. Maybe I could take some online courses or start then take a break I don't know. I don't want to live off yo ass forever," I said jokingly. Even though I was dead ass serious, depending on people never lasted forever. Shit my own mother didn't even take care of me once she decided she didn't want to.

"Shit ma that's good. When do Keyon start pre-school? Just go back now why wait. Life is short no since in waiting. I need to order my little man a book bag. Maybe he could get one of those Gucci shits or the ones with the spikes. I saw a hot ass red and black one the other day." He pulled out his phone I guess to google the two thousand dollar book bag he thought our son was wearing to preschool.

"Kem, about that, he has a book bag already. It has some Batman Lego people on it and he has a matching lunch box. Cost twelve ninety nine at Toys R Us. But feel free to cop me one of those Gucci bags for me to wear to school." I laughed. He gave me a fake sad look. "When he is older you can buy shit like that. Right now cartoon characters are his name brand."

Our food came and we laughed and joked the rest of the time. It was nice. I felt like I got to see another side of Kemori. One where he let his hard ass exterior go for a little bit. As he pulled up to my car I could tell neither one of us wanted our time together to end. "I'm going to come tuck the kids in later if it's cool. I won't stay long I just miss them," he explained.

I nodded before grabbing my purse and leaning over to kiss him on his cheek. "It's cool Kem, come see your kids anytime." I hopped in my car and turned up the heat. I swear this August was chilly with all the rain we have been getting. Once I made it home I thanked Phantom's aunt who had come to babysit for me. I tried to pay her but she refused.

"Sweetie I love me some babies and I get lonely in my house all alone. I will help out anytime you want especially with the new one coming." She smiled at my shocked face. "Us older people always know. I see you are catching up to Inaya." She laughed. I gave her a hug and walked her to her car. Once she left I took off all my clothes which were still a little damp and walked around in my bra and panties. I went upstairs to check on the kids who were both sound asleep even though it was not that late. That's good it gave me time to do what I had to do.

Pulling out Keyon's IPad I logged into my e-mail and located the acceptance letter for Berkley. I was surprised I got in with a GED but I scored so high on their entrance exams they offered me an academic scholarship. I did have to write a letter telling them why I didn't graduate with a traditional high school diploma. I felt like I wrote a damn good letter too. I probably made some people cry on the admissions board.

Logging in with my student information they sent me I went through the process of registering for classes starting August twenty eighth. I was so excited. I had to buy myself some school supplies and make sure I found a daycare or a babysitter for lil miss Kaidence. Enjoying the peace and quiet I laid down on the couch and turned on the TV.

Kemori

Running my hands over my braids I decided to ignore my emotions concerning all this abortion shit. Any other girl and I would have flew they ass first class to the clinic and even covered the bill. Na just had a nigga heart and shit like that fucked me up. I can't say I felt like I saved my baby because honestly I don't think she would have went through with that shit at all. The look on her face when I got there was one of pure agony. She wasn't going to do it. That was one of the reasons I was able to forgive her ass so easily.

I wanted to follow her home after we ate but I didn't want her to think I was being pushy. I made the choice to leave so I wanted her to have her space. I drove around the spots I had checking on all those knucklehead ass nigga's that I had on my team. Rolling up to the building the family ran on 134th I saw Avian's car parked outside. Walking in this nigga was sitting on the couch looking like a commercial on alcohol addiction. "Get up son," I said shaking him.

"What the fuck man," he said jumping up and putting his hand on his nine. I wasn't scared though. He smelled like a bottle of Hennessey exploded all over his ass and his hands was shaking, Looking into his bloodshot eyes I knew I had to reach out and try and help him.

"Avi lets go man. Let me get you home you can't be laid out in the trap all wasted and shit." I did a count of some money and drugs before shoving this nigga out the door and into my car. "You my brother and all but if you get sick in my shit I will whoop your ass." I warned as he leaned out the side of the door and threw up.

Hearing how he was gagging almost made me sick. I threw him a bottle of water and started up the car. I turned on the air even though it was kind of cool hoping that would keep him feeling well enough to make it to his house. "Too bad I'm not your brother," he mumbled almost like he was talking to himself.

"Son, we brothers, we have the same blood flowing through our veins. For all we know Kane punk ass could have been lying and even if he wasn't we always been brothers. Now that Kane ass is gone the Deranjed crew is ours. We got to find a way to run this shit together. Call a family meeting tomorrow and we can start making some different moves. Don't make that shit for the morning though because your heads going to be banging when you wake up. Maybe Za'adore can make you something to help with that."

He nodded his head. "I will call the meeting for the morning. You right we probably really are brothers. I don't believe nothing that sucka ass nigga Kane ever said. Watching him burn up in that house was the best feeling. He was the worst kind of Dad. Man Za'adore won't be fixing me shit. She is gone." He said that shit with so much anger in his tone I could tell she was the reason he was out here getting fucked up.

Pulling up to the house I followed him inside. I was glad Sophie wasn't around to see him looking like something the trash brought in. Sitting down on the couch I waited for him to tell my where his pregnant girl was at. "So what did you do that made Za leave? Was it Lena? I heard she lost the baby you two were expecting was she still causing problems? I swear these side bitches need a handbook with rules and regulations."

"Naw Za was cheating on me and shit. I just snapped and told her get the fuck out. I caught her with that nigga Drue. The one I told you she was having phone sex with. I don't have time for a hoe, at least not one in my crib wit me. Once she has the baby we can do a DNA test and then I don't have to be bothered with her ass anymore. I wasn't really feeling her ass anyway. She was just one of the bunch," he shrugged his shoulders for effect.

"Man you love Za'adore crazy ass and she love you too. Why else a pregnant chick hiding in the trunk of your car all squished up like a sardine. You need stop drinking and fix that shit. Even if you don't want her here you got to look out for little mama she carrying your seed. Plus I knew she was good to Sophie. Don't go out like our pops. Just cop her a house and car. Throw a little bread her way. You just put her out with nothing. Hell you killed her mom so there was no going back there. Does she even know her mom's was in that house?"

I could tell from the way he was looking that he never mentioned killing her mom. "Man I got to go, Nadège ass pregnant again so I am about to go check on her and the kids. Stop fucking up son. I will get wit you tomorrow at the meeting. Go get some fucking sleep or something." His ass was half asleep in the chair when I walked out the room.

Long Island to Jersey was a longer drive than I wanted it to be. It seemed like the traffic on the bridge was never going to end. Finally I pulled up to the house. I sat in the driveway and smoke a little before I went in. Spraying some cologne so I didn't hug my kids with all that weed smoke I jumped out the car to make my way inside.

Using my key I walked into a silent house. Pulling out my gun I felt fear race through my body. It was only a little after seven and no one was making any nose. This was the reason I had to get to Sam. I was tired of worrying about his next move. His next move needed to be black shoes and suit only. Hearing the TV on low in the living room I put my gun away before I stepped in. Nadège was sprawled out on the couch with only a light purple lace panty and matching bra on. Her belly was still flat but our baby was making his or her presence known by making her tired.

I was about to run my hand over her bare skin when I heard little footsteps on the stairs. "Daddy," Keyon screamed waking Na up as he ran into my arms. I tossed him up in the air and gave him kisses. I hated spending too much time away from my kids.

"Where is your sister," I asked as I followed him back up the stairs. He pointed to her room as he tried to pull me towards his. "Hold on let me look in on Kaidence I am coming. I will read you a few stories before you go back to bed." I negotiated. He smiled and ran off to find books I guess. Kaidence was sleeping on her side with her pink and white pacifier in her mouth. Her little footie pajamas were white with pink and yellow ducks on them. I ran my hand over here hair lightly and turned to get a diaper. I changed her and carried her downstairs. I knew my baby wanted to eat.

Na had grabbed the furry throw blanket she kept in the living room and put it around her. I handed her the baby and made sure I lightly touched her breast. She rolled her eyes and I smirked. I stood there watching as she took her full breast out of the bra so she could feed the baby. Damn, I could see the milk leaking out of the nipple before she placed it in the baby's mouth. I was hard as fuck. "Daddy let's go" Keyon said interrupting my thoughts.

I stayed upstairs with my little man for a couple of hours. He finally fell asleep during the second half of the Bee movie. He made us watch it over and over again. Keyon ass needed a bigger bed I realized as I stood up and stretched out the cramps in my legs from laying with him.

Kaidence was back in her room in clean pajamas. She was sleeping on her tummy with her butt in the air. She smelled like baby powder. Nadège always kept our kids fresh. I respected her for that because I see a lot of women have they kids out here in dirty pampers smelling like three day old food. Putting my hoodie back on I walked downstairs so I could leave.

"You bout to go," Na asked me. She was sitting up still in her panties and bra eating something out of a bowl. Walking closer I sat down next to her. She stuck the spoon in my face for me to have some of her black cherry ice cream. That was my favorite. "You going to watch this show with me, I heard it's funny as fuck." She hit he Netflix button on the remote and went to her profile.

"I guess this some Netflix and chill shit," I joked taking my hoodie and t-shirt off. I kept on my marina and jeans I didn't want her to think I was on no slick shit. She set her empty bowl on the side table and clicked on the show Shameless. I heard about that shit too. I usually only watched news and basketball but I would do whatever for her.

"Come here," I said pulling her closer to me. She cuddled up with her back to my chest. I could feel her bare soft skin. I knew she could feel how hard I was but she didn't say shit. After the third episode my hand started to creep down her leg. I was just copping a few feels. Nadège let out a sigh, I could tell she liked how my hands felt.

"Don't worry I can resist ma. But just barely." I whispered in her ear. Moving my hands I rubbed her hair until she fell asleep.

I stayed away from Na for a while after that night. My desire for her was way too strong. I would just pick up the kids and haul ass. All I thought about was bending her ass over and sliding my dick inside of her warmth. I fucked a few girls here and there and I even doubled back to Angalee sometimes but nothing seemed to satisfy me the way I needed. The way only Nadège could.

I decided to slide down to Manhattan later to pick up Na some shit for back to school. She started next week and was so excited every time she mentioned college. I was proud of her she wasn't wasting anytime working towards her goals. I made sure to cop her that Gucci book bag she wanted and some matching sneakers. "Sir are these a gift for your sister," the hopeful sales girl asked me. I could already see the little slip of paper with her number on it in her hand. Shaking my head I proceeded to crush shorty's dreams. Naw, these shits is for my girl. As a matter of fact grab me those baby shoes and the dress to match in a six to nine months and give me whatever new women's shoes you got in the same size eight.

One thing I learned was to not let anyone play on my baby moms. She was not really my girl but she was my world and moving forward she would always get my respect. Miss disappointed made her way to get my purchases in order and wrap them up. I stopped at the Apple store and grabbed my girl a Mac Book Pro, an IPad and some wireless beats headphones. I swear those mother fuckers were trying to sell me everything. I had no clue what she needed all this shit for but fuck it I knew she would be happy.

My last stop was Victoria Secret. I wasn't trying to buy no panties or shit like that I just wanted to hook Na up with those expensive ass sweat suits all the girls be wearing. I grabbed everything I could find in her size and some lotions and stuff. All the women in the store thought it was cute to see me shopping for my girl. I felt like a soft ass nigga. Next time she was just getting some cash.

I made sure she was out when I went to the house. I wanted to set this shit up as a surprise. I found some of Keyon's red construction paper and wrote *Congrats We Love You* on it with a black marker. After setting all the shit up on the bed I propped the little note up and went downstairs to wait.

Nadège came home carrying the baby in one arm and a few bags of groceries in the other. Grabbing the baby I let her carry the bags. "Long time no see. I thought you was out of town or some shit." She looked sad when she said it but her voice wasn't bitchy. I guess she was accepting that we was not really together the same way I was.

Slapping her on the ass she laughed. "Oooh daddy why did you spank mommy, was she bad?" Keyon asked looking at me with his eyes wide. Dam his little ass be seeing everything.

"Keyon go watch TV and stay out of grown folks business." I told him. As soon as he walked out the room me and Na bust out laughing. "That nigga too smart, always watching me and shit like he knows what's up," I told her. "Ma I need you to go look at something I bought for Kaidence. I left it upstairs on your bed. Just want to know if it fits before I get out of here."

"Damn you leaving already Kem. I guess I was bad," she joked as she ran up the stairs.

"Slow down don't be fucking jostling my baby around and shit," I yelled after her. I could hear her screams all the way from downstairs.

"Kem you didn't have to get me anything but I love it all." Good thing I had set the baby in her swing because Na jumped in my arms almost knocking me over. She was hugging me so tight I thought I was being strangled. Then came the kisses, she was kissing my face then her lips touched mine and I lost it.

I had tried to hold back from her but I couldn't. I let her tongue invade my space as my hands made their way up her dress to caress her ass. Damn her ass was perfect, nothing we had to put insurance on because it was real but just perfect for me. I peered over to see Kaidence sleeping and I could hear the Paw Patrol theme song coming from Keyon's room. I knew we was good for a few minutes. I carried her to the downstairs bathroom and closed the door.

I let her body slide down mine and I felt like my dick was going to burst out of my pants. "Girl you are killing me. I need to feel that pussy." I said as I unbuckled my Gucci belt. I yanked my pants down then I started massaging her breasts through the thin green material of her dress. Pushing her gently against the sink I lifted her onto the edge and leaned her back a little. As soon as my hands felt her thong it was soaking wet. Damn she was more than ready.

Taking the head of my dick I rubbed the tip on her clit and watched her squirm. "Yes ma, come all over I want to see you come on my dick head." I was so turned on when she bust and squirted all over. Pushing my way into to her tight walls I felt my knees buckle. This was what I needed, what I been craving. "Throw that pussy," I encouraged her as I grabbed her ass and sank myself in deeper.

"Kem fuck me harder baby. I love this big dick daddy," she moaned in my ears. I pulled out and caught my breathe. Even though we didn't have much time before one of the kids needed us I wasn't trying to be a minute man. Pulling her down I bent her over and spread her pussy lips for a better look. Her clit was throbbing and her pink lips where covered in her juices. Slowly I entered her from the back, her walls clenched me so tight I was seeing stars. Reaching around to rub her clit she went crazy. She was fucking me like a porn star. I couldn't hold back anymore. I grabbed her hips and fucked her hard until I bust in her pussy.

Chapter 8- The grass is never greener
Za'adore

I sat outside of Avian's place with my bags watching the sun come-up, trying to figure out what to do. I fingered the money I stole from Avian on my way out. I knew he always kept cash in his top dresser drawer. While he was sleeping I reached my hand in and swiped the stack. I wasn't really stealing he could consider this shit child support for our son. He told me to leave them put me in his bed. I couldn't take his up and down mood swings. I started walking with the suitcases and my book bag on my back. I knew I looked a mess. I hadn't even showered and my hair was a frizzy mess.

Finally reaching a bus stop I thought about my next move. I wanted to call Nadège and ask could I stay with her but the problem was I didn't want Kemori to tell Avian where I was. This was going to be a fresh start for me and my baby. Picking up the phone I dialed Drue's cell number against my better judgement.

"Hello, who is this," he answered with a voice filled with sleep.

"Drue its Za'adore, can you come get me please? I am at the bus stop across from the Walgreens on Crescent. I need a ride to a hotel. Please." I added the please hoping he would move a little faster.

"Aright man, stay there and I will come and get you." He sounded annoyed but honestly I didn't give a fuck. He played a part in all of this bullshit too. After another forty minutes of waiting he finally pulled up to the curb in front of me. I stood there waiting for his lazy ass to get out and grab my bags. After a few minutes the trunk popped but he remained in the car. I opened the passenger door and sat down making sure to keep the door opened until my shit made it in the trunk. "Yo ma you not grabbing your bags," he asked me with a confused look on his face.

"Naw nigga you going to get those bags. You act like you don't see this big ass belly in front of me. Didn't your mother teach you any fucking manners?" I was annoyed and I only been in his presence for a few seconds. He dragged his ass outside the car and grabbed the bags flinging my shit in the trunk and slamming it shut. Just like a damn kid, I couldn't believe we were the same damn age.

"So where to now Za, what is up with you out here with all your shit anyway? That nigga put you out or something?" He asked with a sly smile. I am sure his bitch ass done figured out I was put out. Why else was I walking down the fucking street with everything I own packed into a bunch of suitcases?

"Yea I was put out thanks to you and the bullshit from yesterday. If you would have just left me alone I would still have a home to go to. Just take me to a hotel, not an expensive one either. Find like a Red Roof Inn or some shit. I am on a budget. He sat there staring at me for a minute like he was thinking of what to say next.

"Za I am sorry I got you put out. I have a place. It's not that big but you can come and stay as long as you need. Or at least until the baby comes, I am not really a fan of kids. They are noisy and smell funny and shit." He pulled off without waiting for a response from me. What kind of man doesn't like kids, I hope he knew we had no future right there. I slightly nodded in agreement. I needed to use the money I took for my baby when he came so I had to do anything I could to save.

I thought we would be heading to the expressway since it took so fucking long for him to pick me up but instead we drove about ten minutes and pulled up to a brownstone. The outside didn't look too bad. We got out and this time mister idiot knew to grab the bags. I followed him into a black gate and to the side of the house. There was a door there hidden behind the bushes. This looked like the door people walk through in scary movies and got murdered. I hesitated and looked behind me to see if someone was hiding in the bushes. "Come on what the fuck you waiting on, ole scary ass," Drue called out.

I followed him down a few steep stairs and realized he lived in a basement apartment. The ceilings were low and the floors looked like they belonged to a traditional basement. Grey cold concrete. The walls where painted a bright white and the one window over the kitchen sink brightened up the place a little. The apartment itself was a wreck. I could tell Drue was one of those niggas that will always need to live with a woman or his mama. There was a stack of dirty dishes in the sink, an overflowing trash and dirty clothes everywhere. I was saying all kinds of curse words in my head.

"I have a spare room you can take from when I had a roommate. I had to kick him out because he was sloppy as hell. I followed him into the bedroom and was relieved there was a carpet, a bed, dresser and a TV. I was grateful none of the mess from the rest of the house had leaked in here.

"When did you kick him out?" I asked with a raised eyebrow.

"Oh he been gone a few months, couldn't you tell it's been a while by how clean the place was?" I was speechless. The roommate probably ran his ass up out of this dump. Sighing lightly so he couldn't hear me I began unpacking my stuff. I told myself I wasn't cleaning the apartment but within a few hours I had the place smelling like bleach and pine cleaner. I had no desire to smell the funk that was Drue.

My first few nights at Drue's were ok. Today I was finally meeting with Nadège for lunch at Applebee's. I was looking forward to seeing her. I was very lonely living away from Sophie and Avian. I wanted so badly to call and ask to speak to Sophia but I blocked him the day I left and didn't look back. I had Drue drop me off before he went to his so called job. I was seriously wondering how he really made his money. He was always around and he would have a ton of secret phone calls. I didn't know if he realized I noticed or not. But every time I walked in to the room he would hang up. He didn't look like a drug dealer but sometimes you really couldn't tell.

"Hey boo," I cried walking in. Na was looking great. Her hair had red highlights and was pulled away from her face with one of those white flowered headbands. She had on a pair of dark blue shorts and a white off the shoulder top. Her perfectly pedicured toes were painted a come fuck me red. Hugging her as best I could with my belly in the way I sat down in the booth across from where she sat.

"I have a surprise for you," she said smiling. She waved to someone at the table near us and I prayed it wasn't Avians behind. Seeing a middle aged Spanish lady walk over with a baby carrier I smiled. Then I noticed the two kids running behind her.

"Mama, I miss you so much. Please come home," Sophie cried as she fell in my arms. I held her in my arms as tight as I could. I smelled her baby smell and then set her next to me. Pulling Keyon to me I gave him a hug too. I was so happy to see my baby. The day went by faster than I would have liked. Nadège just said that Avian was worried about me and asked was I ok where I was at. I told her I was good and fuck Avian. She did have a point when she said I would have to deal with him one way or another.

I found out that Na was pregnant again and started college. I was so proud of her. "So what is living with Drue like," she asked once the kids left with her new nanny. I laughed so hard I almost choked on my drink. "That bad, huh," she said?

"Na he is a slob, I swear I thought Avian was a little sloppy this nigga is a straight up pig. Plus I think he has the wrong idea about us. I found him in bed with me last night trying to play with my nipples and rub on my pussy. I almost took the bedside lamp and bashed his brains in. I explained as nicely as I could that me and him were not in a relationship and that I would never fuck another nigga while I was pregnant. He said he understood but then he grabbed my ass when I left this morning so I have a bad feeling he really wasn't listening. Plus there's just something about his ass that makes my skin crawl. He's always just looking at me with a crazy look in his eyes."

"Maybe you should stay somewhere else," she said with worry in her voice. I shrugged and changed the subject. I was doing what I had to. It would be ok. We started talking about the stuff I wanted for the baby and I had a feeling Nadège was going to go over –board with the baby gifts.

"So what have you been doing now that you're single," I asked her.

"Well I met someone. Girl I almost sliced his ass up over a parking space at a Tim Hortons. He's really sweet though. His name is Grant and he is movie star fine. He dresses kind of preppy but I don't mind. He works in sports medicine helping professional athletes with injuries and shit like that. I mean for right now he's just someone I talk to on the phone. I am going to have three small kids so it may not work out in the future."

"Plus Kemori crazy ass is not letting you date," I said laughing. I was serious as hell. I had Na drop me off at the house and thought about reaching out to Avian. He did let me see Sophie today so I was happy about that. He deserved to know where his son was at. I unblocked him and sent him a text.

Me: *Thanks for letting me see Soph today I missed her like crazy.*

Avian: *Ma where you at? You can come home if you want to I apologize. I should have never put you out like that. Just sometimes my temper gets the best of me. I aint even mad about the money you took. I knew you had to make sure our son was straight.*

Me: *It's ok Avi, you can't force feelings that aren't there. I will be honest with you I am at Drue's spot staying in his guest room. I don't want to be here but I am working on a job and my own place. I really don't fuck with him like that. I have no feelings for him and won't ever be interested in fucking his ass. It's going to take me a long time to get over you.*

Avian: *Aright Ma, I don't like it but shit I put you out so I have to accept it. If you need anything just hit my line.*

I sent a smiley emoji and put my phone away. As soon as we pulled up I was happy to see Drue's car was not parked outside. All the food I ate was catching up to me and I needed a nap. As soon as I thought I would have peace and quiet I heard the grate outside the door. Hurrying out of the shower and in my room I felt violated when Drue just burst through the door.

Clutching the towel over my body I was pissed off. "Yo fucking knock when you come in here. Damn creep."

"Man I aint come in here for all of that. I came to see why you didn't invite your friend in. This your crib too ma so invite Nadège over sometimes."

Over the next few weeks this nigga asked me to invite Na over to the house around fifty times. I was feeling some type of way. Like what the fuck was he stalking my friend? I started applying for jobs but it was hard once the employers realized I was pregnant. I submitted my resume a few more places before closing my laptop with a thud and rolling over to get some sleep.

Slowly opening my eyes I let out a deep breath. I had been having the worst dreams since witnessing the murder's that occurred at Avian's house. I was pissed because it had been a few months and the dreams were getting better and not worse. I had seen people killed before so I couldn't figure out why I was having these dreams or even feeling bothered. I rubbed my hand over my belly in a circular motion trying to get my baby to uncurl from the hard ball in the corner of my belly. My anxiety has been through the roof and the baby wasn't taking it well. I wanted to turn on the TV or the light something to chase away the lingering nightmare but aside from soothing my baby the rest of my body wouldn't move. I couldn't even roll to the side. Fear was paralyzing me and my heart was racing. It was like my mind was in a fog. I could feel the tears dripping onto the pillows and creating a wet spot.

The worst part about the dreams where once I woke up I still felt that feeling of being in danger. I wasn't picturing the dead bodies or anything that had anything to do with that day. I was picturing myself being tortured and beaten, my unborn baby being smothered. I tried to move again and couldn't, instead I cried out. Quickly I clamped my hand over my mouth and rolled on my side. I knew he would be coming soon, his heavy footsteps clunking down the hallway, they even made noise when he was barefoot it irritated my soul. Just like clockwork I could hear him coming, sighing I closed my eyes hoping he would leave. I didn't want his pity or comfort, I didn't want his love, and he wasn't the man I wanted.

"Za you good ma, I can lay with you until you feel better," came his soft voice in the silence of the night. Shaking my head no the tears fall faster as I felt Drue climb on the bed anyway. He pulled me close and I could feel the baby kick the shit outta me. His ass was evil like her damn daddy. She kicked me so hard I almost threw up. Seeing my phone screen light up and hearing a low buzz I knew it was Avian. Who else would be calling me at four AM.

"Hello," I answered as I scooted to the edge of the bed. Drue sat up and sucked his teeth. "Avian what do you want this time of the morning, I am pregnant and tired." I said. Even though I wanted to have an attitude honestly I was just too tired. I had been away from Avian for two months now and it was killing me. But my pride wouldn't beg him to love me or beg him to take me back. Realizing he didn't say a word I started to get annoyed. "AVIAN, what do you want," I yelled.

"Yo lil mama pipe the fuck down. I was just calling because; well I don't know I just felt the need to speak to you. Don't even say now slick shit either or imma find you and fuck you up." Avian said in a voice I haven't heard in a long time. It was that voice that made me think he loved me, that I was special to him. My heart was crying out I miss you but my mind was telling me to not say shit.

"This nigga always calling and shit in the middle of the night like he don't fucking know people trying to sleep. I got fucking work in the morning B, you need to shut this down so we can go back to bed," Drue said talking mad shit.

"Drue why the fuck is you in my room anyway, I didn't ask you to come in here? Stop acting like we are involved in something, you are my friend and I appreciate you but it is time for you to exit my bedroom because I am a whole grown up and answer my phone when I feel like it." I raged. I knew Avian retarded ass was about to have some shit to say so I just held my breath and waited on it. Drue stomped his way out of the bedroom like a small child. Falling back onto the bed I snuggled into the soft pillows.

"Don't worry I aint about to talk about your little situation, hell you have to do what's best for you. Za'adore I just wanted to hear your voice. Stay on the phone ma, don't hang up, I am used to having you sleeping next to me. I need that today." Avian almost sounded like he was pleading. Putting my phone on speaker I listened to him tell me all about Sophie's day and how she was driving the new nanny crazy. I knew I needed to set up some type of visitation because I had no plan on just dropping out of her life. I just needed some time to get over everything that happened. Not long after I fell into the best sleep I had in a long time.

Chapter 9- Say it isn't so

Nadège

"Mommy are you going to school today," Keyon asked as he barged into my room without knocking? I swear he acted more and more like Kem every day. "Well Daddy said he is picking me up this weekend and I can't wait. We are going to see a basket-ball game and then to Chuckie Cheese." I mean this lil boy never got tired of Chuckie Cheese. I was going to be having nightmares about a mouse if he kept that shit up. Stretching out I rolled over and looked at the video baby monitor. At almost five months Kaidence was sleeping through the night and trying her best to sit up and roll over. The nanny I hired, Carmalita, was changing her diaper and singing some song in Spanish. When I started college I had to make a decision on either putting the baby in daycare or having her home with a nanny. I chose a nanny.

"Well daddy can pick you up tomorrow. Today you have school so let's get dressed. I loved the pre-school that we put Keyon in. He was learning to read small words already and could write his name. I only saw Kem when he came to get the kids or drop them off and mostly he did that when I wasn't home. I don't know if he felt guilty about me losing the baby or if he blamed me. Honestly I was in a place in my life where I didn't care. Or I wouldn't allow myself to care. I was getting used to being alone and starting to enjoy life. For once I felt like nothing was going to interrupt my joy.

Grabbing the baby lotion from Keyon's dresser I lotioned him and put on a grey GAP hoodie with orange letters and a pair of ripped blue jeans. The grey Timbs matched perfectly. "Come on the bus will be here soon," I said as I gave him some scrambled eggs and tried to get him to move a little faster. I swear kids just take they sweet time doing everything. I could see a few text messages once I checked my phone. One was from Kem saying he would grab the kids tonight. Another was from this girl I became cool with at school named Quannie. She was asking me to go out with her to some club in the city later on. I hadn't been out in so long so I decided to just say fuck it and go.

I was excited to get out of the house and just have fun. I was young and I wanted to live the life I had been denied because of my fucked up circumstances. After putting Keyon on the bus and spending a few minutes with the baby I had to get ready for my first class. I was taking up Business at Berkley University. Putting on a pair of black tights and a dark blue cable-knit sweater I pulled my hair back into a cute ponytail and added some light make-up. Sitting down wiggling my feet into my blue Ugg boots I was startled when my bedroom door flew open. I fell to the floor trying to jump up. "What the fuck Kem, you don't live here. Ring the bell like normal people." I screeched. Grabbing my book bag and laptop off the charger I was ready to go. But not before giving him a few more dirty looks

"Where the hell you going looking like that? You fucking the professor or something?" He was talking shit while looking me up and down. I knew he liked what he saw by the way his dick was standing up in his black sweats. His hair was in fresh braids and I could tell he just got his goatee lined up. My baby daddy was so sexy to me. "Let me feel that pussy Ma," he said walking closer to me. I backed away with a smirk on my face.

"Nah we good, you can't do this relationship thing remember? Your daughter is downstairs with the nanny. I am sure she would love to see you." I didn't say anything else or let myself get upset. He was not going to keep drawing me in to his web of lust. Winking at him I made sure to bend over and pick up one of the kids toys so he could see what he was missing. I started to ask him what the fuck he was even doing in my house but I didn't have time to argue with him today.

Hopping in my Acura I turned on the heat because it was getting cold fast and whipped out of the driveway. I drove to school in a good mood, sipping my Starbucks coffee and singing along with Beyoncé. I decided at the last minute to stop and grab a breakfast sandwich from Time Hortons. I was so busy trying to get away from Kem I forgot to eat some of the food Carmalita made. As I went to swoop into the last parking space a dark blue Audi cut me off and stole the space. Oh hell no.

"Hey this was my fucking parking space," I yelled while grabbing my blade with my middle console and jumping out of the car. I was pregnant and hungry so he had the right one today. Banging on the tinted windows ready to fight whoever was driving I was shocked when the door swung open and a sexy ass nigga unfolded his long body and stood up.

"Damn cutie calm down. You was gonna cut me over a parking spot? You gotta be one of those NYC chicks." He said putting both his hands up in surrender. His smile was contagious and I found myself laughing.

"Sorry but on the real you cut me off and took the spot. I had my blinker on." I complained with a pout.

"Aright park behind me and let me buy you whatever you was getting. Under one condition thought. I need your number so I can take you out one day." I parked blocking him in and followed him through the front doors. "My name is Grant, what is yours gorgeous."

"My name is Nadège," I responded. Grant was a charmer. By the button down shirt he was sporting and freshly pressed Khaki pants I could tell he was a professional type. After grabbing a bagel with cream cheese and a fruit cup I waved bye to Grant and hopped in my car. Pulling up at school I was still in a good mood. Seeing Quannie already sitting in our economics class I grabbed a seat next to her. "Hey girl you're glowing today who got you so happy." She asked with a smirk on her face. I laughed and told her about my morning. Classes flew by for me today and before I knew it I was home looking through my closet for something to wear to the club.

My phone vibrated across the dresser, looking I rolled my eyes when Kem's name flashed on the screen. "Hey," I answered with an attitude.

"Yo, I won't be picking up the kids until the morning. Some shit came up I got to handle. I will be there early so have them ready." Here we go with the nonsense.

"Kem I know stuff happens especially with the life you live but do not I repeat do not start disappointing our children. You will not like what happens if you do." He could take what I said as a warning or a threat personally I didn't give a fuck.

"Na don't even say that shit baby girl. I know all I did was disappoint you but trust me I won't be letting my little ones down. I told Avian I would go somewhere with him and I forgot. I will see you in the morning." He hung up and even though I was slightly annoyed I didn't feel like he was suddenly about to become one of those dead beat ass dads or something. I went down the hall to let Carmalita know the kids would be home tonight.

"Carmalita I am sorry and I know this is pretty last minute but Kemori will not be picking the kids up until morning. I made plans to go out so I will also not be here. If you cannot watch them I can make other arrangements." I said as she sat in the family room watching some tella novella show.

Waving me off she smiled. " They both sleep at night anyway and all I was doing was staying home catching up on my shows. I will be going to visit some friends tomorrow. So go and enjoy yourself, they will be fine as always." She was really the best. I shot Kem a text telling him he owed the nanny a gift for cancelling with the kids and he sent back a smiley emoji.

Quannie sent me a message saying she would be at my house in a few hours so I ran a bubble bath and shaved my legs. I was not really dressing up I threw on a grey cotton body suit that hugged every curve. I threw a gold Gucci belt around my waist and a pair of gold heels to match. I curled my hair with these new ceramic curlers I ordered and my shit came out perfect. I perfected my look with a grey smoky eye and some natural looking foundation. I was popping my lips in the mirror making sure my red lipstick was on point when I heard the doorbell ring.

I stopped to kiss my babies and went outside to get in Quannie's white seven series. "Ok bish you looking like new money," she said making me laugh.

"Nah you got it boo." She did too in her white lingerie body suit and skin tight jeans. Her heels where silver and looked like something a stripper walked in. Her bundles where flowing straight down her back and her flawless dark chocolate skin was bare of any make-up except her lip gloss.

Pulling up in the Bronx to a club called Emotions I was glad to see they had valet parking. Shit my ass was lazy these days. As soon as we got out niggas was blowing they horns, whistling and hollering our way. I knew we was some bad bitches but the thirst was real. Once we made it inside we found a little table on the main floor and ordered drinks. I could only have a virgin drink but it was ok. The DJ started playing some old school music and that was when I heard *Cash Money Records taking over for the '99 & the 2000.*

I swear just hearing that the whole club got hype. Me and Quannie made our way to the dance floor and started getting it in. I had my hands on my knees while I slightly bent over and began popping my ass like a pro. Feeling someone step behind me I looked up to see a cute light skin dude with hazel eyes. Winking I started grinding and dancing all over him, he grabbed my waist and we danced to the next few songs. Some Reggae music started playing and I decided to whine a little. In the middle of showing off I felt Quannie grab me by the shoulder hard. "Girl your baby father just walked up in here and he looks pissed," she whispered in my ear. *Fuck.*

Deciding I would try to get away from his ass and fast I made my way to the ladies room to pretend I was using the bathroom. I was planning on hiding out in there until Quannie text me that the coast was clear. That dream went crashing down when the bathroom stall was kicked in and almost broke my nose. "What the hell Kemori this is the ladies room," I yelled in shock.

This crazy fucker snatched me out of there so hard I thought I heard my wrist pop. "This the shit you out here doing? That's your new man or what ma," he said while dragging me across the club and right out the front door. I kicked him a few times and I knew that shit hurt because I had on stiletto heels.

"Kem I am grown and you left me so why are we even doing this," I asked in an annoyed tone. Quannie came outside to see if I was good I guess.

"She good, I will take her home but good looking out," Kem said dismissing her as he looked my way shaking his head. The whole ride home I didn't say a word. I sat with my arms crossed and a mug on my face. As soon as we walked through the door we was going to get this shit straightened around. I was so single and not going to be one of many to Kemori. It was either in or out and he made the choice to be out of my life so he had to live with that shit.

I stomped my way up the stairs as soon as we made it home. Once I noticed Kemori following behind me I threw one of my shoes at his head. Throwing myself on the bed I looked at my wrist and I could see the bruises already forming were Kem had grabbed me as he drug me out of the bathroom. This mother fucker was so crazy only he would run up in a woman's restroom in a public place snatching bitches.

"Na how the fuck you gonna do that shit to me ma. You know I love you and you out here rubbing up on niggas in the club. That's not even you." He said sitting on the edge of the bed.

"Kem what does being in love even mean to you, do you know what love is? Have you ever really loved anyone, your mother, your brother? It is all about you, what you have been through, what you are going through. How much money your making, oh yea and how you haven't killed Sam yet. Not because Sam raped me and beat me but because of your fucking ego. Because Sam was the kill you missed, the one that got away." He reached out his hand to me and I could see the tears in his eyes. I was breaking him down but I didn't care. Let him be broken, and then he would know how I felt. I angrily shoved his hands away from me. "Don't you dare try to distract me. I know what comes next, you have your hands all over me then we fuck and nothing changes. Oh and you walk away from me like always. Don't you dare open your funky mouth to say I love you. Love doesn't hurt like this doesn't feel like you are drowning in a pit. You don't lie to the ones you love. Hell do you even love our kids?"

He moved fast and effectively and within that moment I knew I had went too far. "Na did you hit your head when I wasn't here, you are taking me to a place I didn't ever want to be with you. How dare you question my love for our kids, all three of our kids? You were going to kill our child until I came and saved him. Or did you forget." He said through gritted teeth. His hands were clenching my arms so tight I swear they went numb. "Nadège you belong to me, I am never letting you go. Enjoy this break or whatever you want to call this but if you don't want niggas to lose they lives I would suggest you never attempt dating again. You want to watch a movie hit me up. Need money for shopping use the cards I gave you, when you need a good fuck I will already know and be here fucking you. I always got you Na, I will always be there for you even if I am not right here. There is nothing another man has to offer you because I own your heart and your soul. You can say all you want I don't love you but Nadège I do and you fucking know it. You push me the way no one else ever has and I have never snapped on you. I could never find what you give me in another woman, ever. I love you."

" Kem you have to let me go," I said standing up. Suddenly I felt like I wet my pants and my stomach clenched in pain. This was a pain like I never felt before in my life. I screamed so loud I was sure the neighbors heard me. Looking down I could see the blood and I knew I lost the baby. Kem picked me up and rushed me outside so we could make our way to the hospital.

Even though I was less than three months pregnant losing my baby was a hard thing to deal with. I laid in the cold emergency room looking at the bright lights and trying not to cry. I knew Kemori ass was about to blame me. I felt his hands grab mine. "Yo, ma don't cry, we can make another baby," he said causing me to smile a little. The doctor said that sometimes babies just don't make it in the first trimester and since I didn't fall or have an accident it wasn't due to trauma.

Kem walked me to the car and buckled me in. Once we made it to the house he took off his clothes, turned off his phones and crawled in the bed next to me. None of the arguing even mattered in that moment. We had lost our child and needed each other. I curled up to his warmth before I let sleep claim me.

Chapter 10- Only the strong survive

Za'adore

I had to get the fuck out of Drue's house. He was starting to creep me out. I wanted to ask Nadège could I stay with her but my pride wouldn't allow me too. After school instead of coming back to the apartment I went and interviewed for an evening position at Burger King. The manager didn't look too happy about hiring a pregnant girl but I told her I was really desperate for the job and I wouldn't be quitting after I gave birth. Needless to say she gave me a chance and I started tomorrow.

I was now seven months pregnant and moving around was getting harder and harder. I told Avian I would come over after my doctor's appointment Friday to see spend some time with Sophia. I walked to the apartment I shared with Drue. He must not have heard me come in because for once he continued with his phone conversation.

"Babe look I am trying me best to get her over here. What you want me to do go kidnap her? Shit you know her man is crazy as fuck and I am not getting involved in that. Well look nigga if you could do a better job you come do it then," he yelled the last part before slamming the cell phone down on the kitchen counter. I slammed the front door again making it seem like I just walked in. Something about his conversation threw me off. I didn't give a fuck if he had a girlfriend but that seemed like he was talking to a nigga and what bitch was he getting to come over.

I didn't even speak I just took the bag with my food and Burger King Uniform and made my way to the bedroom. All I did these days was eat and sleep. Turning on the TV I pulled up my texts and saw one from Avian asking how my day was. I told him it was good. I wanted to tell him I got a job but I knew the nigga would have jokes once he found out it was BK. Nadège sent a bunch of pictures of baby shit she was buying. She better hope I found someplace to live or she was keeping all of that stuff at her house.

I fell asleep looking at pictures of Avian and Sophia and woke up to arguing coming from the living room. I didn't know who Drue was arguing with but I was getting tired of this shit. I was looking at an apartment closer to my school in a few days hoped I had enough to cover the security deposit and first months' rent. I still had the money I took from Avian when I left.

Deciding to just get up I waited until Drue's company left to go use the bathroom. He was standing outside of my bedroom door when I opened it. I could tell he wasn't expecting me to be up so early and catch his weird ass. "Drue what the hell you listening to me sleep or something," I asked pissed the fuck off.

"Naw I was just checking on you boo. What you doing up so early," he asked in an innocent tone. One I wasn't falling for in the least.

"I am getting ready for my job and just so you know I should be moving in my own place on the first." Hell even if I didn't get that apartment I was out in the next two weeks. I would sleep in a hotel or a shelter because this ole serial killer acting dude was not what was up.

"Damn like that Ma, you just bought to leave a nigga lonely." He gave me a version of a puppy dog face. I grilled him and walked into the bathroom slamming the door. Lotioning my skin with Armani Si I struggled to fit into the black pants I was required to wear. I was thankful the hideous green shirt could hide the fact I couldn't even button my pants. Putting my hair in two French braids I threw the visor on over them and grabbed a jacket and gloves. This winter was going to be a real bitch.

Making my way inside I was greeted by Natalie the manager who hired me. "Good Morning," she said with a smile. Her blonde hair was pulled back in a bun and her little star earrings were gleaming in the light.

"Good Morning," I replied and clocked in the way she showed me yesterday. I was placed at the cash register in the dining room. Because this Burger King was close to a high school it was busy almost all day. My feet were starting to kill me as I cashed people out and argued about what they did and did not order. Barely looking up at the next person in line I said our standard greeting. "Welcome to Burger King can I take your order."

"Za'adore what the fuck are you doing working here?" Avian said in angry voice.

I didn't want to argue with him at my job but I was sure he would see what I was doing. "I am working Avi. What can I get for you," I asked with a smile? I was trying my best not to give him an attitude. We been getting along lately and I didn't want to rock the boat.

"Za I hate seeing you working in some shit like this. What I want is for you to get my son up outta here. I can tell your feet been hurting and probably your back," he said.

"Sir, can you order some food and leave your personal business for another time? Some of us have jobs to get back to." Some middle aged white man commented behind Avian. I could see him turning around to go off on the guy.

"Avi don't get me fired, I need this job to get an apartment. Just order and we can talk tomorrow when I come to the house," I said urging him to behave. He must have saw the desperation in my eyes because he let it go.

"Give me a whopper meal with no tomato extra cheese, with a fry and a coke icee." He threw a hundred on the counter and moved aside. I put in his order and tried to give him his change but he waived me off.

Avian

The next day I picked Za up from her place, well Drue's place a little early. Watching him walk out following Za'adore I didn't know why but I felt like that nigga was off. "Hey ma you want to grab breakfast before the doctor," I asked as she climbed into my black Audi.

"Ok cool," she responded sitting back in the seat relaxing. I took her to this little diner up the road from the doctor. I opened her car door and helped her up. I rubbed my hand over her belly and my son went crazy. She had about five weeks left and I couldn't wait to see my son's face. My first son! Once we were seated Za ordered half the fucking menu. Once the food came she ate all that shit, I wonder if she was eating right. I had to do something about her living situation. Once Kem talked to me about taking better care of her I bought her a house and car. But every time I tried to talk to her about it she cut me off.

The rest of the day went by too fucking fast. The doctor's office for once wasn't busy so we were in and out. I didn't want my time with Za to end. Pulling up in my driveway I almost hated to bring her here. There where so many bad memories for her. She didn't seem to be bothered once she saw Sophie her spirits where high.

They played Barbie's and ate pizza for dinner. Sophia asked for her mama every day. I felt so guilty every time she looked for her. She read Sophia a story before she fell asleep. Slowly she made her way back into the room. "I'm ready when you are," she said yawning.

"Ma just stay here tonight. We can go buy some baby shit in the morning or whatever you want." I could see she wanted to but was scared. "I promise I aint bout to fuck wit you." I reassured her.

She nodded and walked up the stairs. "I got to be home early though because I have work," she shot back.

"Za can we talk about that job shit? I got a house for you and a car. You don't need that job. Please think about our son. I am not trying to push you but just think about it." I begged her before she closed the door to the guest room.

I sat up not able to sleep. Flipping through the channels I heard a scream coming from the room Za was sleeping in. I grabbed my gun and made my way to the guest room. Za was alone but she was crying out in her sleep. What the fuck was going on. I hope nothing was wrong with our son. I put the gun on the dresser and ran to her side. "Bae you ok," I said gently waking her. She sat up with tears and sweat dripping down her face.

"Sorry Avi, that's why I wanted to go home I been having those dreams for a while now. Since the day Kane was murdered. I didn't mean to wake you I should be good now." She said rolling to her side.

I went to the bathroom and wet a rag. Coming back I wiped her face and then got in the bed with her. Sometime during the night her naked body ended up covering me like a blanket. I missed her body and seeing her carry my baby just made me want her more. I remembered all the times I fucked her like a bitch in the streets and wanted to cry. I gently started sucking her breasts and she cried out in ecstasy.

I took my time kissing every inch of her bare skin. Once I made my way to her treasure I slowly stuck out my tongue flicking her clit. She was so wet and juicy. I liked and sucked until she couldn't take it anymore and had an orgasm in my mouth. Trailing kisses up her leg I got behind her. I knew she couldn't do a lot with that big ole belly in front of her. I slowly slid all my inches into her tight ass pussy. I could tell she wasn't fucking anyone else. I was so stupid for so long.

Even though I wanted to just fuck the shit out of her I was determined to show her I could make love. That I really did love her. When I finally came it was the best feeling in the world. I was so weak I couldn't even move.

The next morning I woke up to see Za sitting on the edge of the bed with her head in her hands. "Yo you good," I asked as I got up to take a piss. I could see her hair moving up in down. After we both handled our hygiene and had breakfast with Sophia it was time to take Za home.

The ride was silent, I think both of us was still tired as fuck. I pulled up to see Drue ass walking out the door and waiting at the gate. "Za I don't like that nigga. He seems like he is holding you hostage or some shit. You need to leave his ass ma." Reaching in my pocket I gave her a few grand in cash hoping she would take my offer and move out asap. I wanted to show her I was there for her no pressure of nothing else.

"Thanks Avi, I truly appreciate you. When I can I will pay you back." She leaned over and lightly kissed my lips. I pulled her in closer tangling my hands in her hair and deepened the kiss. Watching her get out and walk in the apartment was the hardest thing I ever did. As she approached Drue it looked like they were arguing. I sat there making sure he didn't put his hands on her. I would have dropped his ass right there in front of his neighbors and all. Pulling down the road I parked and sat there for a minute. I was going back and forth with myself trying to figure out if I should go grab Za and make her leave.

Like a sign from God I noticed she left her house keys on my seat. Grabbing them and making sure my nine was fully loaded I crept out in the early morning and made my way to the door. I learned from Kem to always follow my feelings and this shit didn't feel right.

I unlocked the door as quiet as I could and walked into a small ass kitchen. The air was stuffy because the apartment was in a basement and due to the one tiny ass window it was almost pitch black in there. I could hear men's voices coming from the back so I followed them to a bedroom. The door was cracked and when I looked around the corner I almost dropped my gun at what I saw.

Drue was standing in front of the bed with his nasty dick out and he had a guy in front of him like they were in the middle of some freaky shit. I wasn't shocked he was an undercover I was shocked at the nigga on his knees. It was the one and only Sam. Wanting to bust they chrome right away I waited to hear what they were talking about.

"She cannot leave here today. You need to go and tie her ass up and make her call that bitch Nadège over here. I worked too hard to set this shit up and you not fucking it up for me." Sam was hissing in Drue's face as he paced the floor with only a pair of boxers on.

"Remember I want Nadège when you are done punishing her. I just want to have her in my possession," Drue said in a sick tone. Damn he was obsessed with Nadège how the fuck that happen. Slowly I eased opened the door and shot both those sick mother fuckers in they head. Drue died with his mouth opened ready to scream.

Checking the other room I found Za'adore hiding next to the bed. I guess the gun shots scared her. "Come on Ma, I got you," I said carrying her out of the house. Once we got off the block I called the clean-up crew. "Don't worry they gonna get all your stuff out of there right away. I won't leave a trace of you being there. Call that job and tell them you too pregnant to work. Let me take care of you."

I think my girl was in shock because she just looked out the window. I bet she heard all the shit those crazy mother fuckers was saying. I held her hand as I drove towards her house, not mine. "It's going to be aright." I reassured her. I wanted her to know she was the only one who mattered to me.

Chapter 11- I aint never letting go
Nadège

Ever since Sam was murdered I felt like the weight of the world was off my back. I couldn't believe he was a faggot all this time and then had the nerve to be using my best friend to get to me. I was so thankful that Avian saved her. Today I had a date with the guy I met at Tim Hortons. Me and Grant had been dating for a few months and I was starting to like him. The problem was since we been dating I haven't been able to stop fucking Kem.

Hearing the bell I ran the brush over my edges one more time and made my way downstairs. Carmalita let Grant in so her was waiting for me standing there in a suit and tie. I was glad I picked out a little black dress because he was looking sharp. Seeing the front door open again Kem walked in wearing a pair of Robin jeans and a matching red hoodie, he walked like a boss and his style just turned me on. He said hey and walked upstairs to grab the kids and I was glad he didn't create a scene.

As soon as I turned to leave I heard him calling my name. "Na I can't find the babies chain can you come here and help me."

"Sorry Grant I will be right back," I huffed. I motioned for him to sit while I ran upstairs. "Kem really I have reservations. And why are you looking for Kaidences stuff in my room," I fussed as I walked in.

Suddenly I was grabbed from behind and being pushed against the dresser. "You look so fucking sexy in that dress ma. Take care of daddy," he whispered in my ear. He already had his rock hard dick at my entrance pushing against my scrap of panties. I let out a moan and I guess he took that as permission. Pulling my hair he started going hard and making me squirt.

"Kem hurry up," I said breathlessly. I threw my ass back and rode the wave until we both came together. "Jesus Kem now I gotta clean my damn dress." I rushed to wash up and put on a new little black dress. Walking downstairs I found Grant sitting at the kitchen table scrolling on his phone. He smiled but then frowned when he noticed the outfit change.

"The baby threw up on the other one," I said grabbing my purse and ushering him out the front door.

****

I rolled over on the bed sitting up to see Kem picking up his pants off the chair. He must have washed up already from last nights sex session. The ironic thing was now that I had a boyfriend and he was single or whatever we spent more time together than ever. I felt like Kemori was my best friend. Plus his sex game kept my body on fire. "Damn I can't get the dick before you go?" I said with a smile. I was dead ass though. I needed it day and night, he had me spoiled like that now.

Kem walked over to me and put both hands on the bed. Leaning down he gently kissed me on my lips. He hadn't done that in a while, he said I was probably kissing my man so he wasn't fucking wit my lips. "I would give you another shot of that good dick I know you be dreaming about all day but I got to go. The hospital just left me a message. Angalee's daughter is mine. I am going to head over to the hospital and get my baby. Angalee got too much going on for me. I can't leave my shorty out there to fend for herself. Wit Keyon and Kaidence I know they good because they got a mom like you."

I could feel my body get stiff, even though I pretty much knew it was Kem's baby hearing it for a fact was a blow. I nodded as he threw on his green V-neck Davinci shirt and grabbed his grey hoodie. I wasn't mad at him, shit he could have lied and said he had to handle business. We were not even in a relationship anymore. I just felt hurt because he was the love of my life. No matter what happened or who I met I never loved anyone like I did him. "Kem if you need me just call. I will be around today, going to do some Christmas shopping and stuff."

"Good looking out Ma I appreciate you." He turned to leave. "I got some other shit to do today but I'm going to make it back out here before the kids go to sleep. I left some money on the dresser for you to shop with." I got up and jumped in the shower. I was proud to say I had no tears over the Angalee situation. I didn't feel like her having this baby affected the love me and Kem had, so there was no need for tears. Hell for whatever reason he wasn't even there when she had the baby. I didn't question him or push him one way or another. I was glad he finally came to terms with having another child and making sure his baby was straight.

I hurried and put on a pair of skinny light blue jeans and a red sweater that only came to my mid drift. I threw on some red and white hi-top Vans and went to see what my kids were up too. "Hey mommies babies," I cooed as I walked in to the kitchen kissing them on the cheek. Carmalita made cheese and veggie omelets and fresh fruit with whip cream. She was a doll, not only helped with the kids but cooked and kept things organized. After I sat down and ate two plates of food I figured I should get ready to go before it started snowing. I shot a text to Grant telling him I was on my way to the mall. I was supposed to meet up with him today so we could spend some time together while he was off of work. I was so used to messing with a boss nigga sometimes I got annoyed with Grant's nine to five schedule.

I decided to take the Infinity truck. Honestly I rarely drove it since I loved my car but it was just sitting there in the garage waiting for me to fill it with shopping bags. Adjusting the seat and mirrors from tall ass Kemori I pulled down the visor to check the mirror and a picture fell out and onto my lap. I was almost scared to pick it up because knowing Kem's freaky ass it was probably some butt naked stripper type chick. Flipping it over it was a picture of me and Keyon. We were at the park near Yankee Stadium. I was chasing Keyon and had just caught him. We were both laughing as he was trying to escape my hug. My heart started beating fast and I felt a warmth flow through my body. All this time Kem rode around with this picture of us. He really loved me. I wish he would realize our love was enough. That he didn't have to keep running.

Backing out of the driveway I drove to Palisades's mall. I pulled up to valet parking and jumped out. I was not lazy by far but the air was so cold I was not in the mood to freeze. I handed the valet my car and a twenty as a tip. "Na," I heard someone calling my name. Turning around I saw Grant jogging my way. He had on a pair of Khaki slacks and some black Polo boots. His black leather jacket fit him like a glove. His brown skin was almost red in the cold air. I could see his waves looked neat as always. Leaning in for a hug his Burberry cologne clung to me like a fur coat. "You look good. Let's get inside before you freeze," he said grabbing my hand.

"Ma'am, you left your phone on the seat of your truck," the valet ran up and told me handing me the IPhone 7. Shaking my head at my own carelessness I threw the phone into my purse and thanked him.

As soon as we got inside the mall he snatched his hand out of mine. "Yo whose truck are you driving?" He questioned me with an attitude. Really, why I always get the duds? I tilted my head to the side trying to figure out how to respond to Grant without hurting his feelings or just physically hurting him.

"Grant why does the truck have to be someone else's? I can't have a truck? Hell it's not even a mainly truck. If you must know the Infinity truck belongs to me. I drive it when I feel like it. I prefer driving my car because I don't like parking the truck especially in the city. If you have any other dumb ass questions, please let me know." I turned and began walking, I wasn't here for the shits. He could stand there and argue with himself.

"So Nadège let me ask you another question," he said trailing behind me. He was like a lost puppy following his master. "Did your baby daddy buy the truck for you? Because you don't have a job so I am confused as to how you could afford a truck like that."

Sighing I turned away from the window display at Journeys, I was looking at a cute pair of sneakers for Kaidence. "Listen grant, my children's father had the truck. I liked it and wanted one so he gave it to me. Once I had the baby I needed a bigger vehicle. This was before your time so not really sure why it's relevant or a topic of conversation at this point. In case you're wondering he also bought the Acura and the house that I live in. You are right I don't work because I am blessed enough to be able to go to school and take care of my kids without having to struggle. Don't get it twisted I have money and I have an income coming in. I don't appreciate being talked to any kind of way. I only been dating you a few months so please don't make me regret it."

He stood there for a few minutes quiet. I guess he was picking up his pride off the floor. Ole sucka ass nigga. I can't believe he tried to come for me. That was the problem when you try and date a good dude. One who wasn't psycho or in the streets they turn out to be return to sender ass nigga.

Walking in the MK store I grabbed a few purses I had been eyeing for myself and walked to the register. "I got it," Grant said pulling out his Amex.

"No. I got it but thank you." I paid the sales clerk in cash and picked up my bags. I didn't want any man thinking I owe him nothing. The whole day Grant had a little attitude. He was ruining my shopping trip. "Grant I am hungry so can we go eat," I asked? I was trying to cut the tension and get him to act right. He nodded and I headed to this Mexican restaurant they had on the second floor. I loved their food.

After Grant had a drink he seemed to relax a little and we began talking about current events and what I was learning in school. Looking up I was happy seeing the waitress carrying food in my direction. That didn't last long when I noticed Kem sitting a few tables over with some scrawny ass light skin girl. I hoped he wasn't on a date with that anorexic bitch but the way she was laughing at every word he said I knew he was. He caught me looking at him and grilled me then looked away. I wanted to go beat the shit out of that girl for being with my man, except he wasn't my man.

"I knew you still had feelings for that nigga, shit ya'll probably still fucking," Grant said with an attitude. I couldn't really deny it. I ate in silence knowing that would probably be the last date me and Grant had.

Kemori

Opening the door to Nadège's house that night I could feel my blood boil. She has some nerve getting all angry about seeing me with a bitch when she was out with mister shit head in a suit. I got over her dating but I guess because we was fucking she caught feelings again. She sent me a bunch of drunken mad texts throughout the night.

Walking in I almost didn't want to cuss her out because she was sleeping in the bed with only my t-shirt on. The shirt rode up and was showing her ass. She was lying on her stomach and I even caught a glimpse of her bare pussy. All I could think about was fucking the shit out of her. I nudged her interrupting her sleep. "What Kem," she said rolling her eyes and pulling down the shirt.

"The shit you pulled tonight, what the fuck is wrong with you. Hell you were out with your man trying to check me. You my baby moms, I got love for you. But you don't fucking own me. I am single."

"See Kemori this is what I mean. I am done with you, all the way fucking done. Don't speak to me anymore nothing, have Avian come pick up the kids and leave my fucking key on the dresser. As much as I have your back, give you all my love and then you talk to me like a pop off in the streets. I am fed up. She rolled over and put the pillow over her head.

Snatching that shit off I grabbed her and put her ass in my lap so my face was in hers. "See when shit gets crazy you always running. Stop fucking running, I love you but how we gonna work. I told you today I had to go pick up my shorty. A baby I cheated on you and created. We can't move forward from that." I let my head fall and touch her forehead. "Fucked up thing is ma I went to the hospital to pick up my kid and this bitch Angalee was gone. Left a note talking about if she couldn't have me she was keeping a piece of me."

"Kem I would have loved that baby and still will once you find her. I never once told you I wouldn't accept your baby. Yea the situation was fucked up and it hurt but the baby didn't make you cheat. And if I love you I have to love every part of you. You know the problem you just assumed I wouldn't be here for you so you ran. I am done with Grant and you know what Kemori. I am done with you."

I could see by the look in her eyes she was for real this time. I set her back on the bed and gently kissed her cheek. That was my goodbye.

Chapter 12- There's no me without you and I
Six months later...

Nadège

"Kemori where are we going, I don't like surprises, especially ones you be coming up with." I was serious because Kem ass was super fucking crazy and I aint have no time for it. He grabbed me and pulled me up off the couch. "Girl just go put on the dress I left out for you and come on." He gave me a light push towards the stairs. Curiosity got the best of me so I ran up the stairs to see a cream dress with pink flowers. It was adorable with dark pink flowers and a flared skirt on the bottom. The back was out and the top tied around my neck. I hurried and changed. I swooped my long black hair into a bun and secured it with a clip, letting a few wisps surround my face. I slipped on the matching pink sandals and threw on my iced out earrings and bracelets.

Kemori has been home for six months now and things were different than before. Kem was still rude as fuck but he made up for it by spoiling me and the kids. Plus his women problem stopped being a problem once he realized my pussy was the one he was addicted to. Walking downstairs this nigga had a damn blindfold in his hand.

"Naw boo you not covering my eyes and shit. I need all my senses around you." I sassed before walking to the front door.

"Shut the fuck up," Kem said tying the blindfold over my eyes and picking me up. I had no idea how long the car ride was because I fell asleep. Yea this girl was pregnant again. After losing my last baby this pregnancy meant the world to me and I was enjoying every second of it. Finally we stopped and I heard the car doors being opened.

It was late but we were at some beach. I didn't recognize this one so I knew we had never been here before. I took off my shoes so we could go walk on the sand. Kem thugged out ass had on jean shorts and wheat Timbs with a marina on. He better be lucky I loved that shit.

Once we got close to the water he turned to me and grabbed my hand. "Look Na I wanted to do this with just me and you. Forever I want this to just be you and me. There are no words that can express how my heart really feels but I wanted to try. From the first day I met you all I wanted to do was protect you. I failed a few times, I hurt you even more. I can never apologize enough for that.

I just wanted to let you know I love you. You asked me the day our baby died if I knew what love was. Before you Nadège I didn't know love. But after you and our kids my heart was filled with it. Love is finding the person you get up for in the morning. The one you cry over and can't get enough of. Na I love you and I wanted to ask you would be my wife."

Kem dropped to his knee and pulled out a black velvet box. I didn't realize I was holding my breath until he slid the princess cut diamond on my finger. Slowly I stood him up and put my arms around him. "Only you Kem," I whispered resting my head on his chest.

Avian

I could hear Avier crying for his bottle. I could have left him in his own room and had Miss Peary look after him but my son gave me peace. His soft cries turned louder as I laid on the bed smiling. I made my way to the mini fridge in my room and grabbed one of the glass bottles Za'adore insisted on using. There was only two left so I knew it was time for my baby to go home today. I hated when he left me but he needed his mama, at least for the milk out her titties. Well both of my babies would be leaving. A few months ago I realized it was best for Sophia to live with Za full time too. She was the only mom she had and my life really was drama filled.

My personal phone was quiet even though it was the middle of the night. I changed my number after the bullshit with Lena and Tatianna. Tatianna was a girl I fucked from time to time and somehow she was related to Lena. Hell I didn't know but those two crazy hoes broke in my crib a few months ago. They tied up the nanny and tried to kidnap my daughter. After that I slowed down some on all the woman and drinking. I was starting to get to old for that fast life. Even if Za wouldn't take me back I had kids to straighten shit out for. I was surprised when I found out Kem owned all that legal shit. I been sitting on all this money and only had businesses because my pops left them to me. I had never done anything just for myself. If I die I am leaving my kids money but no legacy. Nothing for them to hold on to and say they dad did that, or that I made them proud.

I had a meeting in a few days with a construction company that builds new complexes and apartment buildings and then sells them. I was going to cop a few and rent them shits out. I may never get out of this street shit but at least I would give my kids something to work with so they didn't end up like me. Avier stopped drinking his milk and looked up at me with his bright eyes. He was my little light skin baby, looking extra white like his mama. After burping him I laid him back down in his crib and wandered around the room. For some reason I couldn't sleep. I dropped down and started doing push-ups. After an hour I didn't feel like working out anymore. Thinking about Za'adore I wanted a drink to ease the loneliness but I fought the urge.

We got along now. I guess seeing her work hard to survive made me see a different side of her. I just didn't know how to repair all the pain I caused her. Maybe I never could, that's one of the reason I didn't even bother trying anymore. I wanted to try again though. I didn't want to be satisfied that Za'adore finally allowed me to buy her a crib and a car. I really just wanted us to be back together.

Picking up the phone I called Za to arrange a time for me to drop off the kids. She was on summer break from school so I was sure her and Nadège was somewhere spending me and Kem money. Seeing her in that Burger King outfit holding her back in pain when she was pregnant fucked with a niggas head for real. "Hello," she answered. Her voice was sweet like a song I couldn't get out of my head.

"Hey ma Avier running low on milk and shit so I need to drop them off sometime today. You gonna be home?" I heard silence. Damn was she going to tell me some shit to make me crazy, like that she was on a date or some fuck shit.

"Avi when you bring them why don't you stay the night. Keep me company or something a girl gets lonely in that big ass house on the hill and I miss you." She laughed but I knew that was her way of inviting me back into her life. I wasn't going to make sure I didn't fuck it up this time.

The End...

Coming soon from Tina Marie

The Way That He Loves Me

Back in the Day

Kahmya

"Kahmya, why are you just sitting there staring at the wall like a fucking retard? Didn't you hear me call your name?" My mother's boyfriend Creek yelled. His voice was like a chain saw. Loud and menacing, but I was used to it. Seeing his face twist into that sick smile, I knew what was coming next. He would grab me by my long hair and drag me off the couch. I was in no way shape or form mentally handicapped or like he said retarded. Traumatized by these people I lived with, yes, but stupid, nah. Feeling the breeze on my neck as my hair became knotted into Creek's fist my body hit the floor with a thump. I forced myself to walk so I wasn't dragged. The last time I ended up with a patch of my hair missing. I had to wear a hat to school for a month.

This shit started when I was eight and Creek first moved in. He would grab my butt or stroke my hair on the low. Now that I was fourteen he was playing a whole new game. I was scared of the day he would go too far. "Get on the bed. I don't know why I have to say shit to you when you know what the fuck you should be doing." He demanded. I got into my mother's king size bed and scooted all the way to the edge. I curled into myself as tight as I could and waited. Creek walked around the bedroom lighting candles and shutting the bedroom door. He was setting an intimate scene like I was his woman and not my mother. I wondered all the time what my mother saw in him. He was one of those dudes that just looked dirty. I mean he was clean, showered twice day and even used expensive ass cologne. But the way he carried himself just made you think bum ass nigga. He was a caramel complexion and stood over six feet tall. His beard was neatly trimmed and for him to be over thirty his body was ripped. Maybe it was the fact that he didn't work, or that he still ate Fruit Loops and watched cartoons all day like a child.

Every day I feel like screaming at my mother and asking her why was she still with this grown man child. But a part of me understood. He was good looking and dated her even though she was a single mom and shit. Around here it was hard to find a man who wasn't on coke, beating you or in and out of jail. But didn't she notice how he looked at me? Why couldn't she see past the fake ass way he played pretend step daddy when she was home? Which wasn't very often, my mom worked nights as a home health aide and went to school to be a nurse in the mornings. This meant I was left home alone with Creek or creep as I thought of him most of the time. I felt the bed dip and I tried to take my mind off of his slimy hands on my body. Creek wasn't raping me, yet. He would just hold me at night and touch my ass, boobs and coochie. I would cry until he fell asleep and I could escape. But I knew it was only a matter of time.

Tonight was no different than usual. He played in my virgin pussy until I felt the wet spot on the back of my pink pajama pants. The one with the white hearts, they were my favorites. Another pair stained, not just with his semen but with the shame of what was being done to me. I felt my tears as I traced my fingers lightly over the pattern of my mother's bed. I took my mind off of what was happening by thinking about Tsunami. He was the boy next door, more like the thug next door. I knew he was on the other side of the wall listening. The walls in these apartments were paper thin. I could picture his face, the smooth Hershey colored skin that was interrupted only by the scars he earned in the streets. Tsunami was sexy even though he was rough around the edges. At sixteen he had lived through more than most adults. It showed in his eyes, they were cold, a dark brown that reminded me of a sky on a stormy day. His attitude, well no other way to say it, was fucked up. He said what he wanted with no remorse. But for some reason he always showed me mercy.

After what seemed like hours but according to the clock on the cable box was only forty minutes I felt Creek's breathing even out. Slowly I slid my body away from his and ran to my room. I grabbed a sweat suit from Aereopostale and locked myself in the bathroom. I looked in the mirror for only a second as I ran the hottest water I could. After scrubbing my body and putting on the yellow capri sweats and matching hoodie I was ready. I slid my feet into a pair of black Nike slides on my way out. Holding my breath I reached for the front door praying there would be no creaks tonight. I stood listening in the doorway for any movement but all I heard was Creek's loud snores. As soon as the door shut and I stepped into the darkened hallway I could sense his presence. This was our routine, five sometimes six nights a week.

"Come on", was all he said as he led me to the farthest corner of the hallway. Even though it smelled like piss and weed this was still the best part of my day. I sat down in the shadows and drew my knees up to my chest. I felt his arms pull me close and I let my tears flow again. We sat there like that for hours, Tsunami holding me and me crying. We didn't speak, we didn't need to. I laid my head on his shoulder feeling safe in his arms until I finally fell asleep.

"Yo shorty you and this fucking hair be making a nigga face itch," Tsunami complained waking me up. I was sprawled out in his lap and my face was snuggled in his chest. I knew his back was hurting because the hallway floor was hard as a bitch. "You normally have this shit clipped up or something ma, what's up?"

I looked down at my hands not wanting to get into details of what I went through with Creek. Slowly I sat up and began stretching. Sleeping in a hallway almost every day was no good on the body. "I just forgot ok, sorry it scratched that baby face you think you have." I tried to brush it off as a joke but I knew that he could read me like a children's book. He started to say something but his cell phone was vibrating. I knew what that meant. It was time for us to go back to our apartments before our parents made it in from work. "Tsu, thank you for this, for everything you do for me. I know I don't thank you enough. Shit probably ever. I wouldn't be able to take this, any of this if it wasn't for you." I reached out to him and wrapped my arms around his waist. At sixteen he was already over six feet tall so I had to look up to see his face. He looked down at me with hooded eyes. It was hard to read what he was thinking.

He took his hand and gently moved a curl out of my face. "He pulled your hair again didn't he," Tsunami asked. His voice was cold, that was the voice I heard him use when he was in the streets. I slowly nodded my head yes, I couldn't lie to him. He was my strength, my safe place, my best friend, he was my everything. "Mya, I am going to kill him one day." His voice was so steady when he said that to me. Like he was describing the weather or giving directions. It wasn't a question it was a fact. I couldn't let him do it though. What if he was killed instead or if he got caught. I could never live with that.

I found a smile from somewhere deep inside. "I will be ok, promise." I said to him as I tried to step out of his arms. He held me closer to him and I could feel his heart racing. I knew I had to go, I knew by now my mother would be home and wondering where I was. We could hear people coming and going for a while now and she was for sure one of them. "I have to go Tsu, you know I am going to get in trouble." I knew his mom didn't check his whereabouts. I guess Miss Sadie just felt like he was old enough to come and go as he pleased. My mom freaked out if I walked to the corner store after dark. All of that concern for my safety out in the world, all the *bad guys* who were waiting in the shadows to get me. It was such a fucking joke to me when the bad guy lived in the same house as I did.

"I can't let you go," he whispered. I didn't know if he was talking to me or himself. He turned me around so I was pinned between him and the wall. I felt my chin being lifted. Before I knew what was happening his lips where touching mine. I thought he was going to be rough but he was gentle. It felt like every kiss I ever read about, or dreamed about. It was perfect. He slid his tongue in my mouth and I didn't know what to do. That was my first kiss ever. He sucked on my tongue, then my bottom lip before he ended the kiss. He was breathing hard, like he was in pain. He dropped his face down onto my shoulder and took a few deep breathes. "Don't ever let anyone else kiss you like that, or at all." Suddenly he let me go and walked away. I stood in the dark corner we slept in every night. I was just standing there for a while. I knew I was going to be late for school and I didn't care. I knew my mom was going to kill me but I didn't care. I needed to think about what just happened. To enjoy the feeling of my first kiss without all of the feelings of pain and fear surrounding me.

Tsunami

The shit with Kahmya was so fucked up. It had been going on for so long now I felt like her mom had to know. Some days when I would see her smiling in Creeks face, hugging him and laughing with him I wanted to rip her head off. She would leave every-night for work without a care in the world. Not wondering if Mya was ok. I didn't have kids yet but I knew when I did mine wouldn't be left up in no house with some random ass man. Me and Kahmya relationship was not a normal one. To the outside world we barely even know each other. My life outside of where we live was not one I wanted her involved with. In school Mya was the quiet shy girl. She didn't have a lot of friends just her cousin Xanaya and her best friends Dana and Lolly. No one really paid her any attention because she always had her face in a book. Mya ass was really smart, she was in all these special AP classes and was even asked to join the debate club at one of the suburban schools. Our school didn't have shit like that. I was shocked they had any advanced classes.

I had been missing a lot of school lately because of business. When I was thirteen I began selling dope for some local dealer named Archie. I sat in this building in the South Wedge and handed fiends dime bags of crack out of a back window. It was dangerous as shit because we was located in an up and coming white neighborhood. The money was good and needed. My older sister had Cystic Fibrosis and even though she can walk and talk and do everything for herself her immune system was weak as fuck and her breathing even worse. My mom worked two good ass jobs just to cover the hospital bills. My pops bailed the moment the doctor said my sister was going to be sickly her whole life. I had to find a way to help out. When I worked for Archie I thought that making ten dollars off of every hundred I sold was making real money. I was cool with making a few hundred dollars a day. It kept me fly and with money in my pocket so I didn't have to ask my mom for shit.

Everything was running smooth until Archie decided to get greedy. I worked one weekend three days straight and when it came time to pay me this nigga gonna tell me he got me later. Now I was a young nigga but not a dumb one. After the fourth day of waiting and me getting the run around I decided to take action. I took a knife from my mom's kitchen set and waited outside of one of Archie's spots. It took some patience but after a few days I caught his ass slipping at just the right time. He was drunk off of Henny and cough syrup, not checking his surroundings at all. I ran up on him stabbing him in the back more than once. He dropped like a stone damn near knocking me down. I took all his money and the three eight balls of coke he had in his pocket. After I killed Archie I didn't sleep for days. They say the first kill is always the hardest.

Since then a lot had changed. I formed a crew, found a connect and became my own boss. Now I pay someone ten dollars off of every hunnit to slang my shit. Only I didn't rent out a crib or nothing like that. I stood on the corner lots of times and so did the niggas on my team. I would still be on the corner myself but I dedicate my nights to Mya. Honestly I loved the thrill of the hustle, the excitement from the fast money and having the resources to do whatever the fuck I wanted. But I love Mya more.

I looked back once more at her, standing in the darkness with her arms wrapped around herself. Walking into my apartment my mom was sitting at the table with her nursing scrubs still on. She was an RN in the NICU at Strong Memorial Hospital. My mom was so beautiful. She still had long thick hair that she wore in a long braid down her back. Her caramel skin was glowing but her eyes looked kind of dull and tired. I leaned down and kissed her cheek and she gave me a tired smile. "Tsu where the hell you coming from this early in the morning, and you not even dressed?" My mother asked while eyeing my grey Nike sweats and white tee.

"Ma he was with his boo from across the hall, Kahmya," my older sister Chania said in a sing song voice. "He spends all his nights making sure she's good." She wouldn't shut the fuck up. If she wasn't sick I would have smacked the shit outta her.

"Who is Kahmya and why haven't I ever met her?" My mom asked with a frown. Why would she care I been fucking half these young freaks in the area for the past few years and she knew it. They call twenty four seven and have even fought each other outside our front door. The one good girl I know, the one I care about and she has an attitude.

"You know mom, she is the one with the daddy who always be looking at my ass and titties." Chania continued.

"Yo that nigga is not her pops and it's not her fault that he be doing that shit. Why don't you go back to your room and watch that Porn Hub shit you addicted to and stop minding my fucking business." I was hot.

"Look, I never tell you what to do but there is something about that girl I don't like. Plus I need you to remember that you're too young to be getting serious with any one female. And as a reminder I am not accepting any babies around here so I hope your using the right head." My mom was really lecturing me about having kids when she had kids with a man who left us.

"Ma I aint trying to disrespect you but I am keeping things going up in here, I make sure we eat when you paying doctors' bills and buying medicine. So respect me as a man. The first day I was sliced up trying to help you survive I earned that. Kahmya is my friend. You don't even fucking know her and you fixing yo mouth to say you don't like her. What don't you fucking like? I care about her and she is not up for discussion, ever." I didn't wait for a response. I walked to my room making sure to bump my nosey ass sister. I love her but she was doing too much this morning.

Jumping in the shower I thought back to the first day I met Kahmya. Long before Creek's punk ass moved in and began terrorizing her. Believe it or not she used to be a force of nature, full of life and tough as hell. I was playing outside one day with my homies and she wanted to join in. I told her hell nah because football was for boys. She pushed me so hard I fell and scraped my elbow. Rinsing off my Axe Phoenix body wash I laughed out loud at the memory.

I stood looking in my closet for a while before I decided to just throw on some True Religion jeans and a white V-neck shirt with blue writing from Buffalo. I grabbed a blue True Religion hoodie and slid it on. I pulled my dreads out of my face and into a rubber band. It was chilly outside for April but that was Upstate New York for ya. Fuck moving out the hood I was trying to move to Miami. Throwing on an iced out cross and some Versace cologne I was feeling myself. Looking threw my closet I couldn't find my blue Timbs anywhere. What the fuck, someone in this house was always touching my shit. Walking into the living room I finally found them under a side table next to the couch. "Chania, I know your punk ass was touching my shit. What you let one of your niggas wear them?" I yelled toward her closed door.

"Fuck you old little head ass nigga. You're a slob that's why you can't ever find shit. I am so tired of you and your attitudes. You need to get yo own shit." Chania bitched as she grabbed her book bag. Hell she was a senior in high school so she needed to get the fuck out not me.

"Both of you need to watch your mouth and get to school. I aint raising no dummies," my mom chimed in. Letting Chania walk in front of me I let the door slam as I made my way to school.

Walking down Hudson I saw a bunch of niggas I knew. After kicking it with them for a few I wanted to handle some business before I hit the high school. One of my little workers named Topher was sitting outside the liquor store serving some crack head. "Yo," I called out to him when he was finished. He jogged over to me. "I need you to hit up Villa as soon as they open and ask for Ty, tell him I need three pairs of those new Jordan's that came out today and that I said let you get one of those shits too. I need a men's size ten, a boys size five and a woman's eight. Cop one of the girly sweat suits to match in a medium. Hit me up at the school once you got my shit." He nodded in understanding and scurried off to do what I said. Topher was a good lil nigga, always had my money right and literally worked twenty four seven.

I never made it to a class I just hung out in the hallways shooting dice and talking shit. Walking into the lunch room I noticed my boys Scar and Beans hanging at a table. Scar had his arm around Xanaya's waist. He fucked with Mya's cousin hard. Any dude that looked her way he was on them. I think he just came to school to watch her ass, ole stalking ass nigga. "What's ups son," I said dapping up my boys and sitting down. I could feel the stares of every freak hoe in Franklin High. My chain, earrings and grill had these bitches panties wet. I could see the stains of pussy juice in they pants as they walked by winking, making they booties clap.

I noticed Kahmya walk in alone. I already knew what Dana nasty ass was doing, but I was surprised Lolly wasn't with her. She looked so fucking pretty. She had on a pair of knock off brown Uggs, black leggings and an oversized off the shoulder brown sweater. She was finally growing into her shape and her breasts were sitting up perfect. Her little round ass was sexy to me. It was just fat enough that you knew it was real. She had her hair down and it looked like she had straightened it. She looked up and noticed me, our eyes met but hers seemed distant. She got a strange look on her face before turning to walk the other way. She found an empty table and sat alone. Pulling out a book she picked at her salad and read.

Xanaya was too busy fussing with Scar to notice Mya. I wondered what was wrong wit her. I knew we didn't really talk in school but it wasn't that she couldn't come to me if she needed me. Topher walked up holding my bags in his hand. I was happy he got all the shit I asked for. He slipped me an envelope with my money as I grabbed the bags. "Good looking out. You took your money right," I asked.

"I did, thanks man. I am about to head back out there. I will let you know when I need to re-up." He made his way back out, focused as ever on making money. Kid's was trying to talk to him and all but he just pulled his hoodie over his head and kept it moving. I didn't know what his motivation was but it had to be strong. I sent Chania a text telling her to come and see me.

"Before you say some dumb shit hold these," I told her handing her the bag with the woman's Jordan's in them. She smiled when she saw I got her the newest shit, just like I always did.

"Thanks little brother," she replied hugging me. I lightly shoved her off of me.

"Yo don't be doing all of that in public. I don't want mother fuckers thinking I am soft." I scolded as I turned my attention to my ringing cell phone.

After texting my ex Nina back and forth a few times I realized Chania ass was still standing there. "What's up, you need some money or something?" I asked trying to get her to move. I was about to go let Nina suck me off in the hallway.

"You didn't hear did you," she said shaking her head.

"Hear about what? You good?"

"About Kamya, I thought you cared about her. Look at her, doe she look ok?" I quickly shifted my eyes to Mya sitting all alone at the table in the corner. A few guys approached the table trying to get her attention but she didn't even look up from whatever she was reading.

"Chan stop talking in circles and just tell me what the fuck happened. I hate all these fucking games you females play. Just say what you have to say and get to the point. I got shit to do."

"You want to know what happened, you happened. You think if you don't say shit to her in this school that people won't find out that ya'll are cool. You feel like no one notices you cop her Jordan's and slide her money just because. This is the hood, people aint got no jobs but to mind other people's business. One of your ex fucks, females whatever she was decided that Mya was the reason you guys didn't work out. She made Mya pay for it. Nina and her home girls started some rumor about her last week. Told everybody she fucked Jamal in the boy's locker room. Now you already know that Jamal fuck with that crazy ass girl Rena. So Rena and her home girls followed Mya to the bathroom and beat her like a dog. I honestly don't know how lil mama still walking they took a big ass lock that was on a chain and hit her until she was huddled in a ball crying."

"What the fuck Chania, you just stood there watching them beat Mya up, knowing she aint do shit." Xanaya went off jumping out of Scar's lap and getting in Chania's face. Xan was crazy as fuck and I was honestly surprised Rena's ass didn't think about her when she decided to fuck with her cousin.

"Come on I wouldn't do that shit so move up out my fuckin face. I saw the shit on video. Hell I thought you all knew already. In the future I will shut up and let you find out on your own. I'm out." My sister flipped her curly brown weave over her shoulder and walked away with an attitude. Xanaya scanned the room looking for Rena, her eyes where narrowed and her shoulders rigid. Angry was not the word. As for me I was beyond pissed. I was struggling with whom to fuck up first Rena, Nina or Mya ass for not coming and telling me she had a problem.

"Xanaya sit the fuck down and chill," Scar yelled as she ran across the lunch room. Rena was sitting at her table eating a piece of cheese pizza laughing at some shit her man Jamal said. She didn't even know what was coming. Xanaya took her hand and chopped Rena in the back of her neck sending the pizza flying and her face smashing into the table. Rena wasn't moving. Her friends decided to back away from the scene slowly. Xanaya snatched off one of her Aldo heels and started pummeling Jamal in his face. I guess he thought he was about to fight back. He tried to grab at her arm but Scar was next to them like the fucking flash.

"Now nigga I know you have more fucking sense than that. If my girl wants to fuck you up sit yo punk ass there and let her or we can arrange some transportation in the form of a black bag." He watched Xanaya for a few more minutes before he grabbed her around the waist and threw her over his shoulder. "You just had to involve yourself right. You so big and bad all the fucking time, well miss big and bad if you hurt my baby imma fuck you up." I could see him squeezing her legs harder than necessary and the tears creeping out of the corner of her eyes. Baby, wow, I couldn't picture Scar with no kids. That dude was disconnected he had crazy on lock and insanity on back up. I don't know who fucked him up in a past life because he really had some shit going on in his head.

Walking over to the table where Kahmya was still sitting reading her book, not even paying attention to the chaos around her I could feel my blood boiling. Some nigga named Mars beat me to the table and leaned over to whisper something in Mya's ear. She giggled finally looking up from her book. She still shook her head no at whatever he asked. "Yo Mars, this me son so I need you to keep it moving." I said making my presence known.

"Oh word, shit I had no idea I never even seen ya'll speak." He walked away looking confused as fuck. I didn't give a damn about his confusion. Shit maybe me trying to not bring Mya into my life hurt her more than helped her.

She looked at me for a second then went back to her book. "Yo come her," I said grabbing her by the arm so she could stand up. I could see her wince in pain the moment I touched her. I snatched her sleeves up and saw the bruising on her caramel skin. Already her arms looked purple and blue. I examined her everywhere I could without stripping her ass naked. "So you let these bitches jump you, walk in here and see me sitting there and don't come to me?" The rage I felt was building in my chest and I knew I would lose control sooner than later.

"Tsu we never talk in public, I didn't want to make shit harder wit you and your girlfriends or embarrass myself. This is high school and this is the kind of shit that happens. I fought back as best I could but four girls with weapons and one me, I could only do so much." She looked down at the floor and I knew she wanted to cry but she was stronger than that.

"Man fuck," I cussed not knowing how to handle this shit. Pulling her close to me I gently wrapped her in my arms. I leaned down and kissed her head. "Shorty stop fucking playing, if you need me anytime anywhere I got you. I don't give a fuck about the bitches I was fucking or anything else. Get yo shit lets go." I demanded letting her out of my embrace.

"I can't leave, I have two classes left for the day. Plus where am I gonna go? Home with Creek? I would rather just be here." She responded turning to sit back down.

I could see people looking our way. I guess I was loud or because it was me everyone wanted to know what the fuck was going on. "I said let's go, for someone who is so smart you sure act stupid sometimes." I grabbed her books and her bag and shoved her in front of me. On our way out the door Nina walked in with a big ass grin watching something on her phone. I could tell what she was watching, the video of them beating Mya. I wanted to fuck her up so bad, I wasn't against hitting women but surprisingly Chania walked over and punched her so hard her jaw cracked. Winking at my sister I picked up me and Mya shoes and left.

Made in the USA
Lexington, KY
24 February 2019